ARABELLA AND THE RELUCTANT DUKE

A SWEET REGENCY ROMANCE

SOFI LAPORTE

http://www.sofilaporte.com

sofi@sofilaporte.com

c/o Block Services
Stuttgarter Str. 106
70736 Fellbach, Germany

Editor: Tiffany Shand.
Cover Art: Covers and Cupcakes.

ISBN: 978-3-9505190-2-0

For Isabella, Dominik, and Nicolas with Love

CHAPTER 1

ROSETHISTLE COTTAGE, CORNWALL, 1819

*L*ady Arabella Astley, sister of the Duke of Ashmore, wished she were better at lying. In her entire twenty-two years, Arabella had never lied. Lately, she'd resorted to lying as if it were her second skin. It was rather exhausting. Her name, which she'd changed to plain Miss Arabella Weston, would take a while to get used to. Her new identity as a governess even more so. Exhausted from the coach ride and dusty from the walk to the cottage, she could not shake the feeling that coming to Cornwall to answer the advertisement for the position of a governess had been a foolhardy undertaking. To top it all, she was being interviewed by a mere girl.

"What do you mean you don't have any references?" Miss Katy Merivale's forehead puckered to a frown. Arabella stared at her in fascination. Wisps of dark hair escaped from the girl's thick, messy braids, and her blue gingham cotton dress seemed a tad too short and had patches at the elbow. How old could she be? Sixteen? Younger?

"Miss Weston?" The girl's voice tore Arabella out of her thoughts. "References?"

Arabella squirmed in the rickety kitchen chair. Of course she did not have any references. A duke's daughter did not need any. But governesses were a different matter altogether. Arabella suppressed a groan. Why hadn't she thought of that? She searched the tiny, cramped kitchen for inspiration.

What an odd place for a job interview. But as the parlour room had been uninhabitable, Miss Katy had explained, the kitchen was the only other available place. She'd led her here as if it were the most natural thing in the world. Arabella had been too stunned to even blink. It was the first time she had ever set foot in a kitchen. She fixated on the chipped crockery on the sooty fireplace's mantlepiece as if they could provide references. Sweat pooled in her armpits. Her maid's rough linen dress was too warm and spanned too tightly around her chest.

She licked her lips and decided that the truth was always the best. "This would be my first position as a governess."

"That's not good. We can't hire you without references." Miss Katy propped both elbows on the table and chewed her lower lip.

Arabella shifted in her chair. "But I do have my report cards here, from Miss Hilversham's Seminary of Young Ladies in Bath." She pulled out several sheaves of paper. "Sorry about the smudge. Some tea spilt on it." Conveniently right over her real name, rendering it illegible. It had taken some dexterity to topple the teacup over in a manner that wouldn't drench the entire document.

Miss Katy's green eyes grew huge behind her glasses. "You had music, arithmetic, science, literature, languages, deportment, dance, art, theatre, and history." A note of awe entered her voice. "And you excelled in all subjects."

"I enjoyed studying there."

"Which was your favourite subject?"

"I've always been partial to the languages and literature," Arabella said.

She spoke three languages fluently and without any hint of an accent.

"What was it like at the seminary?"

Arabella smiled wistfully. "Wonderful." Her years at the seminary with her friends Lucy, Birdie, and Pen had been some of the best she'd ever experienced.

"Did you sleep there?" There was a catch in Miss Katy's voice.

"Oh, yes, it was a boarding school."

"Did you share a room with someone?"

"Yes. My roommate was called Lucy." Arabella smiled involuntarily. "She is like a sister to me."

Miss Katy lowered her voice. "Did you — did you sneak out at night sometimes?"

Arabella lowered hers as well. "Oh yes. Several times. We visited graveyards, and once we went to a wishing well at midnight…" That particular adventure hadn't ended well, for she had fallen into the well. Arabella shook herself. "Back to the position I am applying for. I'd very much like to have this position. Not to offend you, but shouldn't I be talking to your mother?"

The girl shook her head. "Mama is dead."

"I am so very sorry." Arabella drew her eyebrows together. "But shouldn't your father be conducting this interview, then?"

Miss Katy jumped up from her chair. "Papa doesn't have time for things like this."

"Excuse me, but how old are you?"

"I am fourteen."

"Fourteen!" Her precociousness made her appear older.

Miss Katy stuck her nose in the air. "It's just a number. I am the mistress of the house. And I say —" She hesitated, tilting her head to the side, as if weighing up the lack of references with her experience at the seminary. "I say that you get the job. You're hired."

Arabella pursed her lips. "That's wonderful, but I would like to have a word with your father, if that is possible. To finalise a few things."

"He won't be very happy if we disturb him. As I said, he's very busy." Miss Katy proceeded to fill a kettle with water and set it on the stove to boil. "Would you like some tea?"

Tea would be divine. Tea and a bath. And a long nap in her very own four-poster bed...

"Yes, please. I mean, no, thank you. About your father. Surely, five minutes of his time is not too much to ask?" Arabella got up, picked up her papers and paused.

The girl fidgeted and pulled on her braids.

A sharp clanking came from the back of the house, making Arabella jump. It sounded like the hitting of a hammer on iron. Before she could ask what that was, the door crashed open, and the kitchen was filled with havoc and mayhem.

A little girl came shrieking into the kitchen, followed by a boy with tousled auburn hair, who was shrieking with equal force. They ran around the table two, three times, before Katy caught the little one.

"Joy! Robin! Quieeeeet!" she shouted.

There was a momentary silence.

"I say, Katy, I just needed to try out my newest experiment on Joy, but she won't let me!" Robin said after he'd caught his breath.

"No!" Joy screamed with all the full force her lungs could muster.

"Yes!" Robin shouted back.

"Quiet!" Katy shouted over both of them.

"But she won't let me try out the experiment!" Robin threw up his hands.

"Because I don't want to!" Joy crossed her arms and stomped her foot. She wore an odd contraption on her head with several antlers.

"What on earth are you trying to accomplish, Robin Merivale?" Katy asked, sternly.

"It's my newest invention. An invisibility machine! All I have to do is attach that wire there to this wire here, and she'll be invisible!"

"Nooo!" Joy wailed.

"Fine," Robin threw his hands up. "Then give me the machine back. I'll try it on Whitepaw."

"No! Don't you dare hurt Whitepaw!"

"Don't be a goose, no one's going to hurt that cat. Try it yourself and you will see!"

"No!" Joy wailed as if the world was about to end.

"Will you just stop shouting, both of you? We have a visitor here."

Both children froze and turned, wide-eyed, towards Arabella, who clutched her reticule and bonnet. She stared back at them, horrified.

"This is Robin, he is ten. And the little one is Joy, she is four. This is Miss Weston. She is going to be our new governess," Katy explained.

Both children's eyes grew round. Joy's mouth dropped.

"Now, that hasn't been finalised — " Arabella took a slight step back.

"It's as good as decided." Katy set her mouth stubbornly.

Arabella sighed.

Master Robin looked at her, scepticism written all over his face. "Can you teach me about the mechanics of engineering?"

"Engineering? Well...." How to answer that question? It looked like her second round of interviewing had begun, and it might be more demanding than the first.

"Do you know anything about steam engines?" he demanded.

"I have read about them in the paper."

"Aeronautics machines?"

"You mean hydrogen balloons?" Arabella's face brightened. She'd attended a balloon launch with her brother, the Duke of Ashmore, several years ago. "I've actually been in one."

Master Robin's jaw nearly dropped to the ground. "Nooo. You've been on a manned hydrogen balloon flight?"

"I just went up and down, but it was the most exhilarating experience in my entire life."

"You actually were *in* a balloon as it went up?"

Arabella nodded. No need to tell Robin the balloon had risen only a few feet before her brother had insisted to let her down again. Ash had not gone along because he was afraid of heights.

"Capital! What was it like? Were the people really small and the houses and trees and did you have the feeling of weightlessness, of f–f–flying?" he stuttered in his excitement.

"Well, yes."

"Did you know the first man who flew across the channel —"

"Jean–Pierre Blanchard." That much she knew. She'd read an article on him in *The Times*.

Robin's eyes glistened with hero–worship. "It took him only two and a half hours to fly from Dover to France. In a gas balloon. Lighter than air!"

A little hand slipped into hers. Joy looked up at her. She'd taken off the metal contraption. "I'm Joy." She grinned shyly at Arabella. She had a head of unruly blonde curls and dimples in her chubby cheeks. Arabella melted. "I'm happy to meet you, Miss Joy."

"I can read," the girl told her solemnly.

"How very clever of you. What is your favourite book?"

She titled her head sideways and considered Arabella. "Mouse."

"That sounds like a lovely book."

"*The Life and Perambulations of a Mouse* by Dorothy Kilner. Papa reads it to her every night." Katy rolled her eyes. "It's a dreadfully dull book, so Papa has to invent most of the story."

Arabella looked around. Three solemn pairs of eyes looked at her expectantly.

"Does Papa know you've hired a governess? I thought he didn't want one." Robin turned to Katy.

Katy pulled invisible threads from the sleeve of her faded blue gingham dress.

Arabella knit her brows. "What do you mean, he didn't want one?"

"Katy, don't tell me you didn't tell Papa?" Robin rolled his eyes. "She does this all the time you know. She likes to do things without Papa's permission."

"Wait." A pang of alarm went through Arabella. "Are you saying you hired me without your father's knowledge?"

"Um." Katy avoided Arabella's eyes.

"Are you saying your father did not send the job advertisement to *The Times*?" Arabella pressed further.

"Papa doesn't want to hire a governess. Doesn't see the need," Robin explained. "But if you know all about hydrogen balloons, then that's capital, and I don't mind." His eyes brightened again.

"We need a governess. Just look at us. What can I do if

Papa doesn't think of things like that?" Katy muttered and waved her arm about vaguely.

"But, Miss Katy, this is just not how things are done. If your father hasn't consented to this, how could I possibly take the position?" She shook her head regretfully.

Outside, the clanking continued.

"Why don't you just ask him? He's out back." Robin sat down at the table and started to fiddle around with the wires of his invisibility machine.

Katy gave up, defeated. "Very well. He's bound to find out sooner or later, anyhow."

Arabella put on her bonnet and went outside. She followed the clanking noise that came from the back of the house. She heard a baritone voice utter a curse. Then she froze and took a sharp intake of breath. For in front of her stood a man, hammering wildly on an anvil. His thick auburn hair stuck out madly in all directions. Heat emanated from his body. And he was naked.

CHAPTER 2

"Good day. I didn't know we had visitors." The man set the hammer aside, wiped his brow with one rugged bare brown forearm, spreading a line of ash across his face, which made him look even more dashingly handsome. He spoke with a vague Scottish burr. His teeth flashed in a grin, as if he were glad to see her.

A flush crawled over her cheeks and she opened and closed her mouth, unable to find the right words. Nothing at the seminary had ever prepared her for this.

He wore a dirty and greasy leather apron, a pair of equally greasy leather breeches — and no shirt. Sweat glistened on his muscular biceps.

He wasn't completely naked, after all. But still. Aside from some Greek statues, the Elgin marbles which she'd seen in the British Museum, she'd never seen a man in this state of undress before. She had rarely even seen her brother in shirtsleeves. That had been indecent enough.

Arabella spluttered.

"Look at this." Unaware of her discomfiture, he stepped up to her as if they'd known each other for ages. Arabella smelled soot, sweat and something more primeval. "What do you think this could be?" He held an iron contraption in front of her face. It looked like a pair of elongated tongs with zigzag arms. "It's my newest invention. Take a guess." He fixed a pair of intense green eyes on her expectantly.

Out of her depths, she took a wild guess. "A pair of tongs?"

He beamed at her. "Correct!" He snapped the tongs shut so they zigzagged outwards. "It's a most useful invention, as I hope to be able to demonstrate shortly."

"What does it do?"

He snapped it. "All sorts of things." He lifted it to his head. "Take off one's beaver hat, for one. Pick up a satchel from the ground so you don't have to bend." The tongs picked up the reticule that she'd dropped on the ground and lifted it into her hands. "Convenient, eh? Pick up things that are too high on the bookshelf." The iron things zoomed past her face and she took a step back. "Pardon." He grinned. His teeth gleamed white in his tanned face.

Katy stepped up to him. "Papa," she muttered. "Put on your shirt."

"What?" The man blinked at her, then looked down at his apron that didn't quite cover his chest. "Oh. Right."

Papa? Arabella exhaled. *Dear me.*

MR PHILIP MERIVALE, BLACKSMITH AND INVENTOR, THREW A veiled look at the visitor. Who could she be? He couldn't quite place her. She was dressed as a servant but had the demeanour of a lady. Why did he think of white-petalled camellias? She had that same kind of freshness and comeliness about her. The girl was graceful in her washed-out but crinkled linen dress. Tendrils of her blonde hair escaped from a bun that had, once, been tidier, and she stood rather stiffly by the forge, staring at him with the bluest eyes he'd ever seen. They reminded him of what the ocean looks like when the sun rays dapple on the waves.

Dash it, in his excitement about his newest invention, he'd forgotten his manners again. He wasn't used to visitors. What did one do with visitors? Coffee? Tea? Did they even have anything to offer in the house? Should he even offer anything?

He wiped his face with a towel, tossed it aside and pulled on a shirt.

"I suppose introductions are in order?" He held out a rust-stained hand. "I am Philip Merivale."

"Miss Arabella A–Weston." She gave a small nod, then tilted her chin up, ignoring his hand.

He dropped it. Zounds, if she hadn't looked down her finely carved patrician nose at him. She made him feel like an unmannerly country yokel, which he probably was.

"I applied for the position of governess, an advertisement that you posted in *The Times*," she said, pulling out a snippet of paper from her reticule.

Philip took the slip and wrinkled his forehead. "What? Governess? I never posted any ad — Katy! Confound it."

Katy lifted her chin. There was a defiant spark in her eyes. "We need a governess, Papa."

He folded his arms. "We've gone through this." Throwing a brief smile at Miss Weston, he said, "If you will excuse us for a moment." He grabbed his daughter by the arm and pulled her to the back of the shed. The woman remained where she was and looked away, but he was certain she could hear every word of their heated conversation.

"The devil, Katy? What are you up to again?"

"Papa! You *know* things can't continue as they are."

"Why not? Robin's fine at the village school."

"He isn't learning anything there, as you well know. You

said so yourself, a thousand times. Which is why you're giving him extra lessons, with the result that he's very advanced in mathematics, but knows next to nothing about anything else."

"Of course he is advanced in mathematics," Philip said proudly. "I am an excellent teacher and Robin is an excellent student. With those brilliant brains that he inherited from me, I wouldn't expect anything less of him. It's working out very well."

"Papa!" Katy stomped her foot.

"What? It's true. Robin is ten, so what's he going to learn from a governess, by Jove? Deportment and elocution?"

"Fine, so it's not for Robin. You can continue tutoring him yourself. But consider me and Joy!"

"Joy is not even five yet. And she is doing very well. She's already mastered basic arithmetic, bright girl that she is."

"And me? What about me? I don't want to learn mathematics all day, even if it's with you. And I am tired of copying the *History of England*. It's boring. And I'm too old for the village school."

Philip scratched his head as he looked at his daughter. Her cheeks had flushed red and tears sparked in her eyes.

"My friends are all going to proper girls academies and learning how to sew, sing, and paint pretty pictures."

Philip sighed. "I've taught you how to paint pretty paintings."

Katy snorted at him through her tears. "Technical drawings, not proper watercolour paintings."

Philip had to concede his daughter had a point.

"You also said we'd only stay here for a month or two and that we'd return home to London, so I could also go to the academy. And now we've already been here four months, and we are not ever returning to London, are we?" Huge tears rolled down Katy's face. Philip's heart wrenched as he took her in his arms and hugged her tight. She was his eldest and 'pon his soul, he loved her. She was precociously grown up in one moment and a child still in another. And she was right. Katy was learning all the wrong things, and he was rubbish at instructing her in what she'd have to know to get through life as a proper young lady.

He looked over his daughter's head at the woman, who stood by the forge, looking pointedly into the other direction.

"What the blazes are we going to do with a governess?" He hadn't meant to say it out loud. He could see by the twitch of her jaw that she'd heard him.

"She can teach us to be ladies." Katy sniffed.

"I'm sure neither Robin nor I want to be a lady," Philip grumbled. He took out his handkerchief and wiped her face. She took it and blew into it noisily.

"We have no manners at all. Least of all you." Katy was composed again. "Your behaviour is dreadful. And you know it. It's fine if you want to be like that, but I don't want to go through life like a b–b–boor. I want to learn how to be a l–lady." She hiccupped.

He grumbled even more because there was nothing he could say to counter that.

"But deportment and elocution? Bah. How useful is that to a Merivale? I can't with any good conscience agree to that kind of curriculum. Your intelligent mind will degenerate in no time, and I can't have that."

"If I may interrupt," the woman's gentle voice intruded into their conversation. "I have been educated at Miss Hilversham's Seminary for Young Ladies. It's one of the best academies in England. It is not just a finishing school that teaches the gentle arts, but also real subjects of depth. Miss Hilversham believes in educational reform for girls."

"See?" Katy's face brightened. "She went to this superb

academy in Bath and got excellent grades. I saw her report card." She set her mouth in a mulish line. "If you don't hire the governess, then I want to go to the seminary."

"Seminary?" Philip scratched his head again. "This requires further discussion. I suggest we continue this inside over some tea. With biscuits. Or whatever Peggy left for us. Provided my children haven't munched it all up already. Insatiable brood." He affectionately tugged at one of Katy's braids and led the way to the cottage.

The thing to do was to invite his guest into the parlour. That's what those rooms were apparently for. Except the parlour was his working space and looked like it had exploded. Every inch of the floor was covered with parchments, papers, books, and the table equally so.

He frowned at the mess. "To the kitchen," he proclaimed.

In the kitchen, he proceeded to rummage about the cupboards in search of some food.

"Sit down, sit down, make yourself at home." Philip pointed at the rickety chair. The woman sat and watched with round eyes as he set the table with mismatched crockery. "It's Peggy's day off." Dash it, there was no reason at all why he should feel compelled to explain his lack of servants. It was normal for him to work in and about the house. He actually enjoyed it. Well, aside from washing tremendous mountains of laundry in the brook nearby. That he'd gladly leave Peggy to do.

He handed a teacup with pretty red roses to the girl, the best teacup in the house. It had a chip in the rim but then, it was not as though this was a tea salon at Prinny's Royal Pavilion. If she was going to be in his employ, she'd better get used to the fact that their household wasn't the usual one. Not that he was seriously considering hiring her.

"No biscuits, but — ha! We do have some freshly baked bread." He sliced a loaf of white bread into thick slices and placed a pot of jam with a knife on the table, as well as a plate with a slab of butter. Whistling a tune to himself, he boiled the water in the kettle, which Katy had already prepared.

"This is Papa's blackberry jam," Katy informed Arabella. "He makes the best blackberry jam in all of England."

"He cooks jam?" There was such an odd look of surprise on her face that a laugh escaped him.

"Not only that," Philip replied and leaned against the table behind him, crossing his arms and legs. "I also bake bread and am an excellent cook in general. I am also an excellent blacksmith. My grandfather happens to be Scotland's best blacksmith. Hence my accent, you may have noticed." He grinned as he rolled his 'r's.

"Ah. Yes, I did. You have a slight burr."

"But what I am best at, really, is inventing. Like this." Philip pushed the sugar pot towards her. Set over it was a metallic contraption with wires that suspended a spoon.

"What is it?" The girl leaned forward, and a blonde lock of hair fell into her face.

He blinked and tore his eyes away from her temple, where tendrils of fine blonde hair curled above satin–smooth skin. He had an odd urge to tuck it behind her ear.

"Guess."

She tilted her head to one side as she studied the contrap-tion. "I am not sure. It may have something to do with dispensing the sugar."

"Exactly! Precisely!" He watched her flush, which pleased him. "It's a 'sugar-dispenser'. Watch." He wound up a mecha-nism on the side, turning a small handle, and the spoon jumped into motion. It dipped into the sugar, came up again with a pile, jerked to the side, dropping half of the sugar on the table, and dumped the remaining into the teacup that Philip quickly pushed forward.

"How extraordinary!" She bent forward and tipped a finger at the device.

"Of course. I just need to figure out a smoother motion, in addition to getting the spoon to stir in the teacup! It should be possible. Imagine this, if we also had a 'milk–dispensing device' that pours the right amount of milk into the tea, everything synchronised with a water–boiling device where the tea leaves steep, so all you'd have to do is place an empty cup under the machine, and it creates your perfect cup of tea — can you see it?" His excitement was that of a giddy little boy, willing her to understand.

"Oh, yes." Her eyes widened. Was that admiration? He felt inordinately pleased.

"Well, that would be quite an invention indeed. One day I might attempt it. But my *magnum opus* is going to be something quite different, something utterly brilliant, something splendidly —"

"Papa," Katy interrupted. "We were going to talk about employing Miss Weston as our governess."

"Right." He cleared his throat again. "But first, let's have tea. Call in the others, if you please, Katy."

Katy went off and returned with Robin and Joy. Suddenly the kitchen was filled with cheerful chatter, laughter, and then smacking, chewing, and slurping.

Fudge, his children were like little animals indeed, no manners whatsoever. Not to mention himself! Greeting his guest half-naked. Entertaining her in the kitchen. With both his elbows on the table, he bit off a large chunk of his bread — next time he ought to use a little less salt — slathered it with his best blackberry jam — it really was delicious — when he noticed something odd about the girl. Philip Merivale's mind was busy enough as it was, with one half constantly occupied with his current invention, whereas the other tried to fit pieces of a puzzle together. What, exactly, was it about the girl that didn't quite fit? A vague memory niggled at him.

"Joy, wipe your mouth on the napkin, not your sleeve," he said. "And, Robin, don't wind up the sugar-dispenser so much, it'll break the spring." But Robin wasn't listening. The boy let go of the sugar dispensing machine so that the spoon plopped the sugar onto the table. He watched Miss Weston with wide eyes. As did Katy and Joy. Katy's hand motion was frozen midair, and Joy's mouth dropped open, revealing a mass of half–chewed bread.

Frowning, Philip turned to see what had caused such reaction.

Miss Weston sat as straight as a ramrod, not touching the back of her chair. She stirred in her teacup, tapped the spoon noiselessly against the rim to clear off all liquid and set it aside in the saucer. Then, with two fingers, she lifted the cup, her pinkie sticking into the air. Her cup touched her lips, and she never even bent her head, nor her back. After a minuscule, soundless sip, she set the cup down again. She broke off a tiny piece of bread and with the tip of the knife, dabbed some butter on it. Then she ate it. The entire procedure she repeated in the same fashion, minus the spoon.

A memory stirred deeply in Philip. Of a drawing room in a ducal mansion and a woman who drank tea exactly like her. With manners insufferably high in the instep.

"You are a lady." It broke out of Philip's lips.

Miss Weston froze for a fraction of a second, then set down the cup carefully into the saucer. "Of course I am."

"I mean, you are a lady–Lady." This cryptic remark sounded like an accusation, and devil a bit, it was. Philip pushed back his chair. "Of quality." He swallowed. "A noble-woman." He narrowed his eyes.

She did not reply. But when he saw that she set her lips firmly and that she grew slightly white around her mouth, he knew he was right. God's teeth. The woman was as blue-blooded as he was a hot-blooded blacksmith.

Philip set his cup down so hard that it must've cracked.

He was entertaining an aristocrat at his kitchen table.

This wouldn't do at all.

CHAPTER 3

*A*rabella knew something was wrong when a sudden hush of silence fell over the table. She looked up and saw four faces in different states of curiosity staring at her. Her first reaction was to check whether she had a smudge of jam on her face, when she met Mr Merivale's wary gaze. When he stated, "You are a lady," she knew she had given herself away. But what exactly had she done?

And what was wrong with Mr Merivale? The cheerful, flirtatious light that had been in his eyes since the moment they met was replaced by a flinty, hostile look.

Her chest tightened. She laced her hands behind her back for support and cleared her throat. "Governesses are usually ladies of—of—" She searched for the right expression.

"Of genteel backgrounds who are forced to seek employment, either because their families have fallen on unfortunate circumstances or because they have been unable to contract a marriage." Even his voice had changed.

He spoke in a crisp, cool manner.

"Papa?" Joy looked at her father anxiously.

He broke his severe expression and smiled at her briefly.

"If you are done with tea, Joy, Robin, and Katy, you may go outside and pick some more blackberries for me, will you? I'd like to talk to Miss Weston alone."

"I want to stay." Katy crossed her arms and thrust her chin upward.

Philip rolled his eyes. "Very well. But you two, off you go."

There was a scraping of chairs on the stone ground, a scrambling through the door, and the sound of the door slamming outside.

In the silence of the kitchen, Mr Merivale said, "But you, my lady, are not merely of a 'genteel background,' as you put it, are you? You're a noblewoman."

Her stomach dropped.

"How high up?" he pressed.

"My father was a— ba—baron." She felt heat prickle in her neck. Something told her that it wouldn't bode well for her if she admitted that her brother was the Duke of Ashmore. Why, oh why, hadn't she come up with a plausible tale beforehand?

She cleared her throat and tried again. "My father was a baron who fell on — unfortunate circumstances. He, er, gambled the family fortune away. I don't want to talk about it." That was good. Very good. She remembered that her friend Roberta, whom she called Birdie, was a baron's daughter. Her family had indeed fallen on unfortunate circumstances, and poor Birdie was a governess. It was a true story. It just wasn't her story.

"A baron's daughter." His eyes narrowed to two slits of green jade. "Try again. When I addressed you as 'my lady' just now, you didn't even blink. Your father's an earl, maybe? Or a marquess?"

"Does it make a difference?" She lifted her chin.

He threw down the kitchen towel he'd been holding. "Jove's beard. Of course it makes a difference! We are a solid working-class family. I can't have the daughter of a marquess teach my children! That's ridiculous."

Katy's face brightened. "You're a real lady, then? How grand!"

"Baron." It was better to stick to the same version of a lie once it was uttered.

"Katy." Mr Merivale massaged his temples. "I can't have a noblewoman be in my employ as my children's governess. It's beyond the pale."

"But, Papa, it would be so perfect! She's quality and knows all about what a lady should be like, and she can teach us!" Katy bounced up and down in her chair.

Her father groaned.

"It would be wonderful!" There were two bright red spots on Katy's cheeks, her eyes glistened. "Who knows better about etiquette and deportment than a marquess's daughter? She can teach us how to behave."

"Baron," interjected Arabella weakly, but no one listened.

"I said it's not happening and that is final." Philip raked his fingers through his hair. "Marquess's daughter. Bah. Besides, as I keep saying over and over again, I want my children to learn so much more than the superficial arts."

Arabella sat up even straighter. His words pricked her pride. "I am very well capable of teaching the sciences, arithmetic, history, Latin, French, Italian, German, music, drawing and sewing, and, if necessary, dance."

Katy clapped her hands. "Dance, Papa! Then we could finally go to the village balls and actually join in the dances and not always stand around by the buffet."

He looked pained. "It's not only the inappropriateness of class. The thing is really," he swallowed, looked away and then looked frankly into Arabella's face. "The thing is that we currently haven't a feather to fly with." He shrugged. "I can barely afford to pay our housemaid, and she comes only every third day. How the deuce am I to afford a governess who teaches dance on top of everything else?" He waved his hand dismissively.

His talk about money was vulgar. But then, everything about the man was impossible. Philip Merivale was in a category all his own, without any sense of propriety or etiquette. Arabella's mind worked fast. Did she want to work for someone like that? She could leave now and be stranded on the road with nowhere to go. However, she wasn't penniless. She'd had the foresight to bring along sufficient funds to support herself for several months.

She decided to compromise. "Most families need to hire dancing and drawing masters in addition to the governess. With me, you get everything in one."

"So you're a three-in-one offer. Charming." His lips pulled into a lopsided, sarcastic line.

"All I'd need is room and boarding."

Mr Merivale stared. "You must be joking. You are selling yourself under your value."

Was she?

He leaned forward, elbows on the table. "You really have no idea what a governess is commonly paid, do you?"

"Er." He had her there. She wasn't used to dealing with money matters. Why hadn't she researched this better?

"Twenty pounds per annum. No doubt it's a paltry sum to you, but it is a fortune to me. I'd have to sell my horse, and that won't be happening. I'm very sorry." Mr Merivale crossed his arms.

Arabella's shoulders slumped. "I did say room and board is sufficient."

He shook his head. "Impossible. I am the least person to care about things done in bread-and-butter fashion, but even I know this isn't done. I don't want to be saddled with —" he broke off and cleared his throat. "Miss Weston, or m'lady, or whoever you are. I regret that my daughter has misled you and wheedled you into coming all this way to our corner of Cornwall with the promise of a job, but the truth is, there is no job. And even if there were, I must say, excuse me for being so blunt, you're of no use to us. You'd be the last person I'd hire."

Arabella's head jerked back as if he'd slapped her. He'd just told her she was useless.

She had nothing to offer.

Not even to a blacksmith's family. He didn't want her services even if she offered them for free. Tears prickled behind her eyelids.

Arabella held her chin high and allowed the familiar icy veneer of aloofness to fall over her. She was a Duke's daughter after all. "Very well. There is nothing more to be said then."

She got up, picked up her satchel and went to the door. "It was nice meeting you, Miss Merivale. Mr Merivale." She gave him a frosty nod and left.

CHAPTER 4

*A*rabella walked along the dusty road to the village. A veil of tears muted the purple splash of the lavender fields, the blueness of the ocean. Her kid boots stumbled over a stone, and she flung her arms out to regain balance. She staggered to a boulder by the roadside and sat on it to rest.

The empty country road stretched in front of her. Was this the right direction? She should've reached the village by now. It must be almost noontime. She lifted her head to check the sun's position, but it was overcast. Clouds brewed over the sea as if someone stirred them in a massive pot, and an odd stillness hovered in the air as if nature was holding its breath.

She really should've known better. What had she been thinking?

The moment Lady Arabella Astley had seen the charming, crooked stone cottage, framed by pink rose brambles, she'd known she'd made a mistake. That feeling had been intensified when she stared at the thin slip of a girl who'd opened the door. Somehow, she'd imagined a bigger, more elegant house of the affluent gentry. With servants. This was a farmer's cottage without domestics. No doubt Mr Merivale was right. A family like his didn't need a governess.

When she'd sat in the squashed, stuffy stagecoach that took her away from Ashmore Hall, it had first dawned on her she was making a massive mistake. It was the first time that she had travelled without a lady's maid or companion.

Arabella had been squeezed between a fat man who reeked of garlic and cabbage and a dandy who pressed his velvet-clad thighs against hers and smelled overpoweringly of violets. The woman across from her had gripped a basket full of turnips and grinned at her with blackened teeth. "Where ya off to, lovey?"

"Cornwall," she replied in a clipped tone that invited no further questions.

The coach had rattled every bone in her body, and she was tired to the marrow. She had dared not sleep for fear her head dropped on the dandy's velvet shoulder, or even worse, on the man's with the cabbage breath.

There, in the coach, the rushing high that had flushed through her when she crept out of Ashmore Hall that morning, with nothing but a satchel and a purse full of coins, slowly dissipated. Reality hit her square in the face. Running away in her maid's clothes wasn't just a mistake. It was a disastrous decision that she was going to regret for the rest of her life. If anyone ever found out, her reputation would be in tatters.

Her entire life she'd had to focus on maintaining her reputation. She'd had a lonely childhood in Ashmore Hall, raised by her grandmamma, since her mother had died at her birth, and her father wasted himself away with wine, women, and song. Her overprotective brother wouldn't let her take two steps out of his sight. He'd been more a duke than a brother, and she'd languished in his shadow.

If her brother knew... Arabella shuddered.

But, 'pon her soul. This feeling of freedom!

Closing her eyes, she took a deep breath of salty sea air, mixed with freshly cut grass and lavender. She'd never felt so free before.

Here, she was no longer Lady Arabella, sister of the powerful Duke of Ashmore, whose life was predetermined down to the stockings she wore. She was Miss Arabella Weston. For her, anything was possible, because she no longer had a reputation to lose.

She felt a pang of regret that the job with the Merivales hadn't worked out. She'd been charmed by the lively children. They weren't working class, that was certain, even though the father seemed to be a blacksmith– inventor. Middle class was more likely. Either way, it was simply not the thing for her to live with the family as a governess. She had no chaperone, he had no wife, there was no housekeeper or other female servant around. It was highly inappropriate for a lady to spend even five minutes alone in the presence of a gentleman.

But Mr Philip Merivale was no gentleman.

Arabella blushed as the image of his tanned, sweaty arms invaded her memory. Followed by a feeling of deeply burning shame. What was it he'd said?

That she was the last person he'd hire.

She felt an ice-cold stab deep down. For he'd confirmed what she'd feared her entire life. That besides her lofty, noble status, she had nothing to offer to this world.

Arabella, the duke's daughter, was pretty, had a good figure, a fair head with curls that curled in the proper places, the aristocratic Ashmore nose and forehead, a pleasant smile, and graceful demeanour. The *ton* considered her to be a diamond of the first water. She could wear a hemp sack, and it would look perfect on her. She was accomplished in all the arts that a duke's daughter was expected to be accomplished in.

She was, in one word: boring.

One warm summer afternoon, as she was having tea with her friend and sister-in-law Lucy on the veranda, Arabella had realised what was the matter. She'd opened an éclair and stared at the sugary, hard shell. It was empty inside.

This is my life. The thought jolted through her. *This is me.* A hard-sugar shell. And inside: nothing.

She crumbled the éclair between her fingers to fine dust. A gust of wind puffed the sugar dust away. There was nothing left.

Beads of sweat had formed on her upper lip. There was Lucy, chattering on and on about London and the theatre, while she was experiencing the deepest existential dilemma.

Me. What about me?

Then, even more terrifying was the question: *Who am I?*

Arabella felt a black mass stir inside her. It made her want to scream. Like so often in life, she'd ignored it and swallowed her feelings.

When her eyes had fallen on the newspaper advertisement announcing a position as governess in faraway Cornwall, Arabella thought that that would save her.

Run away. Reinvent yourself.

Find yourself.

Prove to herself and the world that she was more than an empty sugar shell.

And that was why she'd taken the stagecoach to Cornwall.

A fat raindrop splattering on her nose tore her out of her reveries. Where had those rain clouds come from? Where was she? She had to return to the village inn to catch the stagecoach to Launceston. Then on to Bath. Back to Miss Hilversham. Beg her to take her in and to help her obtain a proper position as a governess. Maybe she could teach there.

Like Birdie, who, after a short stint as a governess, had returned to teach at the seminary. The thought of seeing her old friend again made her quicken her pace.

A tremendous boom of thunder rolled through the sky, making her jump.

And then the rain came.

CHAPTER 5

*P*hilip Merivale prided himself on being a cheerful, even-tempered man who acted fairly towards his fellow human beings. He also liked to think that he was capable of maintaining his cool in even the most challenging circumstances.

Had he panicked when the two hundred fifty cannons of Napoleon's Grand Battery spewed fire, death, and destruction right at them?

He had not.

Philip had stood his ground, gnashed his teeth and stuffed cotton wads into his ears before he charged with his Baker rifle. The rest of the slaughter was a blur of mud, smoke, blood, and scorched flesh. He'd served in Captain Eversleigh's Light Company of the 2nd Battalion, Coldstream Guards. Miraculously, he'd survived the blasted war. His comrades, including the captain, did not. He'd never gotten over the guilt of being the only survivor in his company. If it hadn't been for his rambunctious three children, he would've gone mad with guilt and grief. As a freshly widowed father, he had no time to dwell on the war. He had a family to care for. So, he'd pushed the memory of war aside as best as he could and focused on the present. Which worked, most of the time.

His time with the Guards led him to think of himself as a man who never made any unreasonable decision born out of a choleric disposition.

Ergo, it bothered him considerably that he'd just cast out a young woman in a fit of unreasonable temper, simply because she was of noble stock.

That wasn't like him.

Philip moodily stirred the pot of blackberry jam. He should be working on his newest invention instead of hiding away in the kitchen, but he couldn't focus. He'd discovered that making jam usually helped him get his mind back to what was essential. As a result, they had more jars of blackberry jam in their pantry than they could possibly eat. The jiggling, purple-black mass reminded him of the girl again, whose eyes had widened when Katy had told her he cooked jam.

A grin flitted over his face. Her expression had been priceless.

She'd been reserved about her background, but he wondered what had really happened that she found herself in such a situation. What girl with her breeding willingly left her family to live with complete strangers who were beneath her station, to make a living? It was very likely she didn't have a choice; despite the Banbury tale she'd dished up. Baron who lost his fortune, bah. It was none of his business, really, but something must've happened for her to resort to such desperate measures. And here he'd never even given her a chance but sent her back to the streets again.

A pang of guilt shot through him.

Her simple dress couldn't camouflage that she was of quality. This had been more than clear by her manners, comportment, and her speech. Her speech! Philip could've banged his head against the stony kitchen wall. Why hadn't he realised that from the moment she'd opened her mouth? He must've been too distracted by her eyes and pretty figure. Only the upper class talked in that posh, elevated manner. He despised that accent with every fibre of his soul. She was also a terrible liar.

Philip frowned as a niggling sense of suspicion reared its head. Who was she? What had brought her here? And why the deuce was he still thinking about her when he'd already sent her away?

Blast it, his children did not need a governess. They had done well all these years without one. He'd have to try harder to fulfil Katy's needs. Very well, so she wished to learn more than how to calculate the speed of a balloon when it rises. Maybe he could ask whether the mayor's wife would be so kind as to teach his Katy a thing or two about how to behave properly in society. Curtsying and fluttering with the fan and all the feminine arts that ladies needed to know. But that was as far as he'd go.

He'd show the world that the Merivales could get by very well without a governess, thank you very much.

Especially if that governess had sparkling blue eyes and a proud tilt to her chin.

Something stirred inside him.

He supposed he was hungry for the jam.

Thunder crashed as loudly as the cannonballs over the fields of Quatre Bras.

No. Louder.

He dropped the ladle and dollops of scalding jam splattered on his arms. Another boom.

Jove's beard. He hated thunder. He hated any kind of loud, sudden boom that reminded him of the war.

Philip picked up the ladle and gripped it hard, his

knuckles sharp and white. A sheen of sweat formed on his upper lip and his heart pounded in his chest. This was how he'd felt before he was about to charge. The sweetish stench of death already wafted through his nostrils.

It was only the jam, charred at the bottom of the pot.

He blinked, shook himself and shoved the pot away from the stove. "It's just thunder. Lightning produces a vacuum, and air rushes in it to prevent its collapse. It's the motion of air that makes such a racket. Almighty Jove. When is this going to stop?" Rain poured down in violent gusts. He peered out of the window and could barely see the trees outside.

"Katy!"

"Yes?" The girl stuck her head into the kitchen.

"Watch the little ones. I'm going to take Hector and the cart. I have to rescue that woman before she drowns in the storm." Squashing his hat on his head, he muttered, "Or dies of fright."

"Capital!" Katy's face brightened. "Is she going to be our governess after all?"

Philip grumbled.

Another deafening clap of thunder made him jump.

He swallowed, then braced his shoulders and went out into the storm.

CHAPTER 6

$\mathcal{A}$rabella clung to a tree. She knew it wasn't a good idea, because she'd been told never to take shelter under a tree during a thunderstorm.

Only if it was a beech. Then it might be safe. Never an oak. These you should avoid. Or was it the other way around?

She prayed that she stood under the right tree. Otherwise, heaven help her.

Death by storm.

Arabella gave a hollow laugh. She'd always assumed her final demise would be in a canopied, down-feathered bed in an elegant mansion, surrounded by her grandchildren. She'd raise her wrinkled hand in a final blessing and then close her eyes as she'd peacefully slumber off into the afterlife.

Instead, she was going to perish under an unidentifiable tree somewhere in Cornwall. Struck by lightning or drowning in a torrential downpour.

She could see the headline in the morning paper: 'Nameless Woman tragically dies in the storm'. Her brother would read it and never know it was her.

That thought filled her with sadness. Poor Ash. She'd never even said good-bye to him.

The rain came down harder. Her dress was plastered to her body within seconds. Arabella could barely see her hand in front of her eyes. Her teeth chattered, and she clung to her satchel as if it was the only thing left in this miserable world that she could hold on to.

Did she hear the clatter of horse hooves underneath the din? She peered through the curtain of rain, but the branches kept whipping into her face and hindering her view.

"Blast it, woman, I knew you were going to be idiotic enough to stand under a tree," a baritone voice roared, which sounded like it belonged to Philip Merivale.

Her heart leapt in an absurd manner. "Where else am I supposed to be taking shelter? In the ditch?" she shouted back.

A tall figure cut through the grey sheet of water. He grabbed her by the arm, and they stumbled to the road, where a horse and cart stood.

"I calculated the probability of you taking this road and the chance of you rushing over to that tree as soon as the storm broke. I was correct in both instances. Didn't you know trees are excellent conductors for lightning and that it can be fatal to stand under a tree? Every child knows that."

Her thoroughly soaked leather boot slipped in the wet mud. Philip caught her and hauled her up into the seat. "Sit up here and pull this over your head. There." He pulled an oilskin over her that smelled like mildew, but it kept some of the rain off.

"That's why I tried to stand under a beech!" Arabella had to raise her voice to make herself heard. "Lightning doesn't strike beeches."

"Old wives' tale!" He picked up the reins, and the horse trotted uneasily down the road. "Besides, that's not a beech, but an elm. Hiya, my good Hector, home as quickly as you can before we all drown in this miserable weather."

A crack of thunder exploded right above them. Philip swore and dropped the ribbons. The horse came to a standstill.

"Mr Merivale?" Arabella cast him a worried look. What was wrong with him? He sat there stiff and frozen and stared into the distance. He did not blink as the water rolled down his cheeks. "Sir?" She shook his arm.

"I–"

"What's the matter?" Arabella shouted into his ear. "Let's go!"

"It's so — loud."

"Yes. That's because it's a thunderstorm. It's only the air moving into the vacuum that creates the noise," Arabella shouted.

He gave a hollow laugh. "Who told you that?"

"I learned it in Mr Keating's Natural Science class at Miss Hilversham's Seminary."

"You are a woman full of mysteries, Miss Weston." His teeth chattered, and he shivered.

Arabella looked at him surprised, then pulled herself together. She had made it this far. She refused to die now. She took the ribbons from his hands and flicked them. "Hiya, Hector," she imitated him. The horse started moving. Thank goodness. She was driving a cart!

"I — Thank you. I don't like thunder, you see," he said gruffly. "Sometimes it reminds me of — you know." He looked away. Rain kept drumming on their heads, but it didn't matter now. Arabella waited patiently.

"The war," he mumbled.

"Oh!" A rush of understanding filled Arabella. "Of course. Beastly war. There is no reason whatsoever to be ashamed of being afraid of thunder. We're all afraid of something. I myself can't abide —" she cut off midsentence.

"Can't abide what?" He leaned forward to hear her better.

She cleared her throat. "It is somewhat embarrassing to admit."

"Come, come. You just said that fears are nothing to be ashamed of."

She felt a light blush rise. "I don't like little crawly animals."

"Crawly animals?" He cocked his head to the side. "Insects?"

"Spiders. Horrid creatures. So there." She giggled. "I've never been so wet before." The rain kept drumming on their heads but somehow, it didn't matter.

The cart rumbled in front of Rosethistle Cottage, and Arabella pulled back the ribbons.

Mr Merivale jolted back into the present as if registering only now that they were sitting in the rain. "Right. Let's get into the dry."

He jumped down and held out his hand. She grabbed it, but he prevented her from descending. He pulled her towards him, so she was on the same level as his odd, green eyes. They had rusty flecks in them.

Rain dripped from the rim of his hat.

"Tell me one thing, Miss Weston." His voice was low, and he held her hand in an iron grip that hurt. "As for those fibs you told earlier today—I want the truth now. Will you swear to tell me the truth?" She nodded.

"Did Morley send you?"

Frowning, she tilted her head aside, which caused rain to drip directly onto her face again. She spluttered and wiped it away with a hand. "Who?"

"Morley." A touch of impatience laced his voice. He gripped her hand even tighter.

"I've never heard the name. Who is it? I answered your daughter's ad in the newspaper. It is the truth."

He stared at her for a moment longer, his lips pressed to an uncompromising line. Then she saw him transform within a second. The stubbornness of his chin relaxed, his eyes widened and crinkled in the corners, and a look of ruefulness entered them.

"Of course, you wouldn't know. But I had to ask. I needed to know whether I could — trust you."

"Of course, you can trust me." Arabella's voice was breathless.

They were frozen in time. Arabella stopped feeling the rain and the cold wind about her. All she saw was that man whose eyes lit up with an inner light when he smiled.

Something flipped in her stomach.

"Room, board, and eight pounds per annum," he announced as he held out his hand.

It took Arabella a moment to realise he was giving her a job offer. She grasped his hand without thinking. "Deal."

"Welcome to the wondrous and chaotic home of the Merivales, inventors extraordinaire. You will come to regret it." A boyish grin lit up his face. "But let's get inside now."

Arabella stepped across the threshold of Rosethistle Cottage.

"And Miss Weston."

She turned. He'd taken off his hat and his dark auburn hair was plastered to his head. He looked bashful.

"Thank you." He didn't wait for her reply but turned to take horse and cart to the safe shelter of the barn.

She knew what he was thanking her for. In some way she felt she'd rescued him, when it should have been the other way around. A warm feeling pooled in the pit of her stomach.

"You are welcome, sir."

CHAPTER 7

In spite of looking like a half-drowned rat, the girl bore herself well. Philip had to admit, she'd surprised him. She'd neither whined, cried, nor complained. When he had one of his "fits," as he called them, those moments when he froze up, catapulted back in time where all he saw and heard was the sound of war, death and mayhem, she'd neither panicked nor fallen into a fit of hysterics. No. She'd taken the reins and calmly led them back to the cottage. She'd surprised him and made him smile. And she'd sworn that she'd indeed answered his daughter's ad.

Philip did not trust her entirely. One was wise not to trust strangers. Not until she told him the full truth of who she was and why she was here. But he was relatively certain it had nothing to do with Morley.

He looked across the room to where Miss Weston stood, drying her face with the towel that Katy had brought her.

"I think we need to have some tea again," Philip concluded, wringing out his hat.

"How absolutely marvellous you have come back." Katy beamed. "But, Papa, where is Miss Weston to sleep?"

41

He hadn't thought of that. Rosethistle Cottage didn't have a guest room. "Good question. The servant room — we do have one somewhere, don't we?" He trudged down the hallway, past the kitchen and opened a small door. The room was so tiny it had only space for a narrow bed, a small nightstand, and a wooden trunk. The window was a small square in the wall. He used this room as storage for his half-finished or failed inventions, and there were many. The bed and floor were littered with his things.

He picked up a wiry device, and his face brightened. "What have we here? My clothes folder. I thought I'd misplaced you for good." To Arabella he explained, "It folds my shirts. You place the shirt on top and do this." He pulled the handle, and the wires folded down sideways with a snap.

She jumped, startled.

"It's not perfect, but in the absence of a servant, it does the job." He snapped the wires again.

"Remarkable." She blinked, looking adorably confused, as if trying to visualise the device replacing a valet.

Philip laid it aside and scratched his neck. He couldn't very well put her in this wee room, could he? Even Peggy had refused to sleep here and preferred to hike back to the village, where she stayed when she was done with the work at the cottage.

"I can move in with the other two, and Miss Weston can have my room," Katy offered.

"That is kind of you, Katy. But I would prefer you to stay in your own room." Arabella opened the door wider and inspected the chamber. Then she nodded. "This will do very well for me. If only you could procure me some linen, a pillow, and a blanket?"

Philip eyed the lumpy mattress with a frown. "Are you certain?"

Arabella examined the room once more and nodded. "I will feel very comfortable here."

"Very well, then. I will see what I can procure in terms of fresh linen." He left to search the cottage for the stated items.

PHILIP MERIVALE HAD SURPRISED HER YET AGAIN. HE'D NOT only cleared out the room in an instant, but brought down a pile of fresh sheets, pillows, and blankets, in addition to hauling from the attic a massive wooden chest that he deposited on her bed.

"I suppose you need to change into something dry," he said gruffly.

"Take out anything you need from there."

Katy, who'd slipped into the room with Joy, gasped. "It's Mama's box!"

Mr Merivale wrinkled his brow. "Yes, it is."

Katy opened the lid and folded back the cloth that covered the contents. It was full of dresses. "I remember Mama wearing this." She took out an India–blue shawl and held it to her nose. "It was her favourite. It still smells like her. Roses."

Mr Merivale fingered the shawl absent-mindedly. "It is a shawl I bought for Jenny with my first salary. How long ago that was." He looked lost.

Arabella saw tears rise in Katy's eyes. She felt a rush of compassion for her. "This is kind of you, Mr Merivale, but I don't think I can accept this. The content of this box belongs to the girls."

"The way I see it is as follows. First: you seem to have nothing to wear other than the wet rag that's plastered to you —" His eyes went to her chest, but he tore them away quickly. Warmth pooled at the pit of her stomach, leaving her confused. "If you don't change into something dry soon," Mr

Merivale continued, "you'll get ill and catch your death, and we can't have that, not when the children are counting on you being their governess. Second, we have a box of women's clothing lying about that no one is using. Third, the owner of this box has no use of these clothes." He turned to the girls. "Having established these facts, we conclude: these clothes are best given to you. Katy, Joy, would you agree that Mama no longer needs these?"

Katy nodded with the shawl pressed to her face. Joy wrapped herself in a forest green strip of cloth, like a mummy, and did not respond.

"Would you agree it would be better for these clothes to be given to your new governess, before they get eaten up by moths?" Katy nodded again.

"So then. It's all yours." Mr Merivale smiled as if he'd cast a Solomonic judgment.

Arabella shook her head vehemently. It just didn't feel right. "I will gratefully borrow one or two dresses since my current dress is indeed completely ruined, and I, er, have misplaced my own bags. But only if we may also refashion some of them for Katy." Not that she'd ever done that before because all she'd ever done was embroidery. But it couldn't be so difficult, could it? She'd watched countless times how her abigail had adjusted her dresses, and she was good with a needle.

Katy's face brightened. "Oh yes! Oh, let's!"

Philip threw her a quizzical look. "If you insist." He lifted a cream– coloured garment and looked at it, puzzled. It was an unmentionable, a pair of stays.

Arabella flushed scarlet.

Katy giggled.

He dropped it like a hot coal. "Well, then." He cleared his throat and didn't seem to know what to do with his hands. Then he unwrapped Joy and hauled her on his shoulder. She

44

squealed. "How about we leave these two to their business and you and I, Jollykins, continue reading Mouse?"

"A mouse! A mouse!" Joy screeched as both left.

A while later they heard his voice droning from the bedroom as he read to Joy and Robin with dramatic intonation.

A wistful little smile played about Arabella's face. How lucky those children were. Her father had never treated her with such evident love as Philip had for his children.

"Miss?" Katy dug deep into the box and dragged out its entire contents, spreading everything on the bed. "There are some dresses in there that mother never wore. Like this one." She lifted a dark blue cotton dress.

"Mama never liked it, because she said it looked too severe on her."

"Perfect." Just the kind of thing a governess would wear.

"This one, too." She held up a forest green dress that went with the shawl that Joy had wrapped herself in. It was a long-sleeved dress for cooler days. "I never saw Mama wearing this one. Or this one, either." She held up a brown dress. "Mama preferred the pink and yellow ones. This one was her favourite." She held up a rose–pink afternoon dress embroidered with pink buds.

"How pretty, Katy. Should we alter this one so you can wear it?"

Katy hugged it to herself. Then she dropped it. "No. It reminds me too much of her. We can use this one." She held up a lemon-yellow dress.

"It would suit you nicely, indeed."

Katy stared at the pink dress. "Mama wore this dress when —"

"When?"

"Oh, nothing." She threw the dress down again. "Mama died at Joy's birth; you know. Joy never even knew her."

45

"I am so sorry," Arabella whispered. "That is terrible. My mother also died at my birth."

"Oh!" Katy looked at her with huge eyes. "So, you never knew your mother."

Arabella shook her head.

"I was as old as Robin when she died. Robin was six. He can no longer remember her face." She looked up. "But I can. She was pretty." She hesitated before she added, with a lowered voice, "but I don't think she was happy."

So Mr Merivale's marriage had been unhappy. Arabella searched for consoling words.

"Maybe you can try to paint the image of your mother in one of the water colouring classes that we will have."

Katy's face brightened. "It is wonderful to finally have a governess."

Arabella hoped that she could fulfil the girl's expectations. Poor children. Poor Mr Merivale.

As she helped Katy refold the dresses, she wondered why she felt like her bones were melting every time Mr Merivale threw her one of his keen, swift glances. It was as if he penetrated her veneer and saw right through to her very heart and soul.

CHAPTER 8

*E*arly next morning it had stopped raining, and a pale sun ray peeked through the tiny window of Arabella's room. She'd slept fitfully on the lumpy, narrow bed but had awoken with a sense of anticipation. This was her first day of work.

She would prove to herself and, most importantly, to Mr Merivale, that she could do it.

Arabella scrambled out of bed and washed her face with cold water from the pitcher that stood on a small nightstand. She pulled on a petticoat and over it a stay. It was an old–fashioned, short stay that laced up in front. Without the help of a maid, she couldn't put on the usual stiff stays that laced up in the back, the kind that Mr Merivale had hauled out of the trunk yesterday. She'd placed it aside for later use. When she heard repetitive clanking outside, she realised he must be already up and working.

She passed the drawing room and noted that the door was closed. Before retiring, Mr Merivale had insisted that they keep away from it until he cleared up the room. In the meantime, she was to teach the children at the kitchen table.

The delicious smell of pancakes filled the house.

Arabella's stomach growled.

Entering the kitchen, she came to a halt. "Goodness!" she exclaimed.

For the cook, standing on a chair in front of the stove, holding the heavy iron skillet in his hand, was none other than Robin. The apron was doubled and tied around his waist.

Robin looked over his shoulder and nearly toppled off his chair. "Good morning, Miss Weston. Just in time! We are having the world's best pancakes."

"You're cooking? Don't you have a cook? And where is your father?"

"Papa's outside. Peggy won't be coming the next few days, so we have to cook for ourselves. Today is my day."

"What do you mean, today is your day?"

Robin, a fold of concentration on his forehead as he held the heavy iron skillet with both hands, somehow manoeuvred the pancake onto the plate without dropping it.

Arabella jumped forward to help him, but he managed to cope himself.

"We each have a day. Yesterday was Papa's day. The day before was Katy's. Today is mine. And —" he beamed at her, "what would you know? Tomorrow's yours!"

Arabella's mouth dropped open. "You mean I must cook?" That hadn't been part of the job description. This house had an alarming lack of servants. Was she expected to fill this lack?

"Good morning, good morning, good morning, good morning." Philip strode in, and suddenly the room seemed too small. "Ah. Miss Weston. I hope you had a good night's sleep?"

"Like a log," she replied. She watched how he washed his

hands in a pitcher, then went over to Robin and planted a kiss on his forehead.

"Robinkin. This smells divine." He sniffed the air. "A bit burned." He helped Robin set the skillet aside.

Katy and Joy entered. "Good morning, Miss Weston."

Philip sat down, and Joy crawled into his lap, popping her thumb into her mouth as she watched Miss Weston. "Ah," he said, "I see Robinkin has cooked us some delicious — beef-steak with kidneys. What are we waiting for?"

Katy rolled her eyes.

Arabella stared at the half-burnt pancake in front of her and opened her mouth to ask where the steak was, when it clicked.

"Excellent — beefsteak, indeed. Very well done." Arabella chewed on a piece of charred pancake but was surprised that if one disregarded the burned bits, it did not taste too bad.

Philip investigated a piece on his fork before popping it into his mouth. "Well done. In the truest meaning of the word."

"You have to add mint sauce over it," Robin said and pushed a jar of blackberry jam towards her.

"Mouse!" Joy contributed to no one in general.

"This is the best beefsteak I have ever eaten." Arabella said. Then she remembered what Robin said before Philip entered. She put down her fork.

"Mr Merivale, am I to understand that it is my turn to produce, er, beefsteak with mint sauce tomorrow morning?"

"Indeed," Mr Merivale replied with full mouth. He swallowed and took a big gulp of a glass of milk that Robin had poured out for them all. "I forgot to mention that."

"I don't think that cooking is part of a governess' curriculum," Arabella replied stiffly. The problem was that she had no idea how to cook.

Philip set down his fork. "Oh. I see." A gleam of speculation entered his eyes. "I see I have to clarify. We Merivales are a working-class family, in case you haven't noticed. You may think this is shocking, but we work very hard for our food. We also cook. We make our own beds. We also clean. And when Peggy's not around —" He bent forward with a diabolical look in his eyes. "We have to wash laundry. With our own hands. In the brook."

Arabella swallowed. "But... but... none of these are part of my skillset. I have never cooked, cleaned, or washed laundry." She wouldn't have an inkling of an idea how to go about doing any of it. "Piffle. Even Joy knows how to cook."

"I cook very well," Joy informed her.

"I am sure you do," Arabella replied.

"I cook — Mouse!"

Arabella nearly choked on her pancake. Robin spat his milk over the table.

"Robin, really." Philip wiped up the mess, picked up Joy and placed her on her own chair, where she proceeded to draw a face on her pancake with the blackberry jam. "We will read Mouse again tonight, child of my heart," Philip assured her.

"Um, Papa, I think she means there is actually a mouse." Katy pointed to a corner. "Over there." Indeed, a little creature scurried behind a cupboard.

"I will get out my mouse traps after breakfast. Special ones that don't kill. But first we need to finish this conversation. You were saying, Miss Weston?"

Arabella sat tensely on her chair. Not only because she was piqued about her expanded role in the household, but also because there was a mouse skittering about somewhere.

"I was saying I know neither how to cook, nor clean, nor to wash laundry." Her nose was in the air. She was a governess, but she wasn't a servant. There was a distinction, wasn't there? Arabella folded her forehead into a thick line.

Her governess, Miss Dowster, had been an in–between creature, neither here nor there. The servants had thought her proud, and Arabella remembered overhearing the housekeeper saying Dowster put on airs and wasn't welcome in the servant's hall. She'd never joined them for meals. It would have been inconceivable for Miss Dowster to have breakfast on the same table as the Duke of Ashmore. To them, she'd been a servant. How must she have felt about this?

Arabella swallowed.

She dropped her head as she realised she'd never bothered to think about what her old governess might have thought.

Philip leaned back in his chair and looked smug. "Unfortunately, Miss Weston, if you are to be the governess for a working-class family, you have to abide by our rules. Peggy isn't here this week, so we all have to cooperate to put food on the table and get things done." He bent forward.

"But I know what your real problem is."

"What?" She couldn't think under his steady scrutiny.

"You think to cook and clean is beneath your station." A line of derision played about his lips. "You are a lady, after all." He linked his fingers behind his neck. "And for some reason, you've chosen us as your social experiment." There was a quarrelsome spark in his eyes.

Arabella sat up, stung. "I did not!" Truth was, in some sense he was right. It was a bit of an experiment for her.

Their eyes locked. He'd thrown down a gauntlet. That was a challenge she could not forego.

"I will do it. Tomorrow is my day?" She looked at Robin. If that 10–year–old could produce burned pancake for breakfast, then, by Jove, so could she!

"Tomorrow is your day. Mind you. That is in addition to" — Mr Merivale swept an arm to his children who ate, oblivious to the adults' conversation— "teaching the brood."

"I will succeed." She narrowed her eyes at him.

He smirked.

She'd show him, she would!

"We will see, Miss Weston. We will see." He looked pleased as if he'd just licked all the cream out of the bowl.

CHAPTER 9

*T*hree pairs of eyes stared at her.

She was their governess. She was to teach them. Except she'd never taught anyone before, and all she was capable of now was staring back, as her mind drew a horrifying blank. She was woefully unprepared and had no idea of what to do or how to begin.

The children sat at the kitchen table, a massive thing hewn out of oak, with knots and deep furrows in its surface. They'd cleared off the breakfast dishes, which were piled up in a wooden tub by the stove. Someone was going to have to wash them. She hoped it wasn't to be the governess.

"Er." She rubbed her lower lip with one finger, pulling off a flaky piece of skin, as she tried to recall what her teachers at the seminary had done on the first day of school.

Joy wiggled in her chair, rubbed her eyes and yawned.

Robin pulled out a pocketknife and began to carve something into the table.

Katy jabbed him with her elbow. "Stop it," she hissed. To Arabella she said, "You might want to see what we know already and compare it to what the girls in the seminary know."

Arabella's face brightened. "Yes. Of course."

"I'm not a girl," Robin growled.

"Certainly," Arabella said hastily. "It would never occur to me to compare you to a girl. But seeing where you are all at is a good idea." She looked around searchingly in the kitchen. "Do you have anything we can use as a blackboard?"

Robin shrugged. "Write with chalk on the table?"

"We used to have slates," Katy looked around as if they were going to appear in the kitchen somewhere. "What happened to them? I'll go look for them." Katy left the room.

"Robin broke my slate." Joy sulked. "Robin always breaks my things." She looked like she was about to burst into tears.

"I do not!" Robin was outraged. "Besides, I needed them for an experiment. Of aeronautical nature. But it's a big secret." He jutted out his lower lip and crossed his arms.

Katy returned, carrying two slates. "There are only two old ones here," she informed them. "Papa must have forgotten to buy us new ones."

"What about books?" Arabella thought she'd seen a book-shelf in the parlour.

"Mainly Virgil, Cicero, and Horace." Katy shrugged. "Which is odd, because Papa hates Latin, and the rest of us don't have a command of it. Oh and there's the *History of England*, which is as exciting as mud."

"I think mud is exciting," Robin muttered.

"It makes nice squishy sounds," Joy agreed.

"It also flies well. You can do lots of other things with it." He looked at Arabella with a speculative gleam in his eyes. Arabella made a mental note to be vigilant the next few hours and check her bed and shoes for mud balls.

"Very good, Latin from the very basics. What about any of the languages? French? Italian? German?"

The three faces stared at her blankly.

"I'd love to learn French. It's such an elegant language," Katy said brightly.

Arabella felt encouraged. At last, something that she could offer, even though Robin was pulling a face and muttering how he preferred mathematics and natural sciences. "What about mathematics, Robin?"

"I know how to calculate the speed of a balloon as it rises. It's easy as pie." He proceeded to rattle off some numerical combinations.

"Dear me." Arabella was out of her depth.

The children's knowledge was disproportionate to say the least. In arithmetic, there was nothing she could offer. Katy calculated with a swiftness that astounded her. She was well beyond the level of mathematics Arabella was capable of. Robin, too, nearly at his sister's level, solved her problems with a yawn.

"Easy as cherry pie, Miss Weston," he said. Their father had taught them, so that would explain it.

Their knowledge of history was disproportionate as well. They knew the Napoleonic battles by heart, down to each battalion's movement on the battlefield, yet only a smattering of Greek and Roman history, and their knowledge of geography could be improved upon as well.

Most importantly, she'd have to teach them manners.

Joy, in the meantime, had lost her interest in the lesson, slid off her chair and sat cross-legged on the floor.

"Mouse, mouse, come out of your house," she chanted quietly.

Arabella sighed. "What about you, Joy? Don't you want to join us here?"

Joy ignored her and sprinkled some cheese bits that she'd kept in her pocket on the floor.

Arabella wrinkled her forehead. What would Miss

Hilversham have done? Threatened, coaxed, or cajoled? She'd been strict and kind at the same time. No one had dared to disobey her during lessons.

"She's only just learned her ABCs with Papa," Katy explained, while Robin proceeded to whittle into the table. "She doesn't have any schoolbooks, though. Papa is great at inventing stories."

Robin yawned so loudly his jaw cracked. "Well, an hour is almost over, and we've done no-think." He laughed at his own wit. "Do you get it? Nothing– No–think." Then he sat up straight as an idea occurred to him.

"Miss Weston, why don't you tell us the story of your balloon ascent?"

Before Arabella could reply that she might do so later if he stopped hewing up the table, Joy emitted a shrill shriek, making her jump out of her skin.

"Mouuuuse!"

Lured by the cheese, the rodent finally decided to come out. Robin flew out of his chair and went after her. "Grand, I can use it for an experiment. I'll make a mini balloon and have the first mouse fly to the moon."

"No, Robin, this is *my* mouse! Don't touch her!" Joy scuttled after it on all fours, trying to catch it.

"It's not!"

"It's so!"

"It's not!"

"I'll tell Papa!"

"Children!" Arabella shouted, but no one heeded her. The mouse zoomed out of the kitchen. Robin and Joy scampered after her, shoving each other out of the way, in an attempt to catch her first.

"Robin, Joy, come back here!" Katy rushed after them.

Within a second, Arabella was alone in the kitchen. She slumped into the chair.

Well, that had been a disaster.

She'd known teaching and disciplining children was hard. But this exhausting? They hadn't even spent a whole hour together. They were not even as awful as she'd heard from other stories — they were bright, lively children. She couldn't even handle that. Arabella wiped her brow with her sleeve.

Maybe she wasn't cut out to be a teacher.

She balled her fingers into a fist, so her nails cut into her palm.

"You will do this, Arabella Astley," she growled. "You *will* not give up. You will succeed."

What she needed was a plan.

Just in that moment, a tremendous thump and a scream emerged from the parlour.

"Miss Weston, come quickly! Joy is burning down the house!" Robin shouted.

CHAPTER 10

The velocity of this device would depend on how smoothly the circle was wrought about its axis. Philip gave the wheel a spin. Excellent, excellent. With the second attached wheel, which needed an additional dollop of oil, and the attached bar between the two wheels, it looked like half a waggon. He tested the wooden triangle attached on top of the bar. Maybe he could come up with a better design. A saddle of some sort. Covered in leather. He sketched a quick design on paper. He'd ask the carpenter in the village to do this for him. Philip was good at working with fire and iron, but he wasn't as adept working with wood. He cracked his knuckles with satisfaction as he studied the design.

By Jupiter, he was a bloody fine inventor.

He wiped his hands on his apron and surveyed it with satisfaction. He'd send a prototype with his grandfather, who was arriving in a few days, to London, to patent it. This was going to be the invention that would make him, that would bring him not only money, but also fame. Not that that was what he really wanted. He just wanted that his inventions actually made a difference to the world. Not silly sugar dispensers, shirt folders, pick up devices and so forth. Mind you, he'd sent in prototypes and patents of all these devices to the London patent office — they groaned every time they received one of his letters, a clerk once told him — which was excellent.

They should know his name, by Jove.

He rubbed his hands.

He wanted to accomplish something bigger than a wee, tinkered device.

He wanted to create something that could change the world.

Like steam engines. Or the voltaic pile. Or gas lamps. Or stand-up baths. Though he thought he could probably do better than what was in use so far. If one could have the water pumped in pipes and warmed before one stepped into the bath ….

Philip's mind whirled with mathematical figures, equations, drawings, and prototypes.

He drew his brows. He'd get to all that eventually. But first, he'd have to make some blunt so he could pay that governess of his. He'd go to the village first thing tomorrow morning.

How was she faring? he wondered. He'd been working outside in his forge since dawn. It was mid-morning, and thirst scratched at his throat. Returning to the house would provide him a good opportunity to check how that governess was getting along.

A smell of something burning wafted into his nose.

Philip crashed into the parlour. The table with his designs was turned over, and his papers and books scattered all over the floor. Katy held Joy, while Robin jumped around Miss Weston, who crouched on the carpet with a scarlet face and blew on burning sheaves of paper.

Instead of putting the fire out, she'd made it burn stronger, as her breath caused the flames to leap higher.

"What the devil are you doing, woman?" Philip tore a blanket from the sofa, pushed her aside and threw it over the burning heap, smothering the fire. He stomped on the carpet to put out the embers. The fire died, leaving a scorched hole in the middle of the carpet. "Haven't I expressly prohibited anyone to be in this room until I have had a chance to clean it up?" Some of his most precious inventions were in here. He cursed.

"It was an accident, Papa!" Katy cried. "Robin was chasing Joy, she turned over the table, and the scrolls flew across the room! Some slithered right into the fireplace, where the coals were still glowing, and they relit the fire. A piece fell on the carpet, and it took light."

Philip paled. "Good God! Are any of you hurt?" Heaven forbid if anything had happened to them. The house could've burned down. His children… he swallowed.

Katy shook her head. "We're fine."

"My work!" He stared aghast at the pile of ashes.

"I'm so sorry, sir. I tried to put it out right away." Miss Weston looked like she was about to burst into tears.

"What did you do while my children were busy setting my house and my entire life's work on fire, Miss Weston?" he asked coldly. "Drink tea and do embroidery?"

"I, uh, well." Arabella sat up and struggled for an answer.

Cold fury gripped him. "How can you leave my children unsupervised?"

"Indeed." She swallowed. "I shouldn't have let them out of my sight."

"No, you should not! Not even for one second. Not even for half a second. Not even for —" Philip took a big breath and controlled himself. "If I had known how incompetent you'd be, I would never have let the children out of my sight, as they normally do their lessons with me in the workshop."

She handed him the charred sheet. Philip groaned. They were the diagrams he'd intended to send along with his inventions. It had taken him weeks to calculate them. Weeks of work. Weeks of sleepless nights of scribbling, calculating … He was about to have an apoplexy.

"Miss Weston," he said. "You are dismissed from this post."

Miss Weston blinked back tears. "I am so very sorry," she whispered. She got up and left the room with quiet dignity.

"But, Papa, it's not her fault!" Katy cried. Joy burst into noisy tears. Robin stood in a corner and hung his head.

He didn't listen. His inventions! Burned! He got down on his knees and picked up the pieces and tried to puzzle them together.

He growled. One paper was completely gone, but it was not the one with the main formula. That main paper had merely scorched corners. He breathed a sigh of relief.

"I only wanted to save Mouse!" Joy wailed. She'd caught the mouse and clutched it between her hands. It squeaked.

Robin sniffed. "I'm sorry, Papa. It was my fault. I shouldn't have chased Joy, then she wouldn't have crashed into the table, and your papers wouldn't have burned. I'm sorry Miss Weston has to leave because of me." He blinked rapidly and wiped his nose on his sleeve.

Katy huddled on the sofa, drew up her legs and wrapped her arms about them. "Things never work out for me. We finally have a governess and then this happens." She wept.

Philip looked up and sighed. Clearly, he'd overreacted. For the second time in two days. That wasn't like him. What was it about that woman that made him lose his calm? He recalled that stricken expression on her face. A tear had hung on her eyelash like a dewdrop quivering on a leaf of grass.

"Come here," he said gruffly and pulled Robin and Joy into his embrace. He took them over to the sofa, where Katy still cried, and hugged her as well. "You gave me such a fright. Everyone unhurt? No burns? Nothing crucial roasted?"

Joy showed him her finger. "Mouse bit me. But it's not bleeding."

"Oh dear." Philip inspected it. "We shall have to invent a special cage for Mouse. What do you say?"

"She's too little anyway for my balloon. I will find something else," Robin said graciously. "Maybe a monkey."

There were steps in the hallway. Miss Weston had put on her spencer and bonnet and clutched her satchel. She looked pale and composed, but her eyes were suspiciously red.

"Where do you think you're going, Miss Weston?" Philip let go of his children and proceeded to collect his scattered papers. "I'll have the room cleared in a minute, then it will be ready for use. Minus the carpet. That's a comfort you'll have to do without for the time being."

Arabella blinked. "But you dismissed me, sir."

"Bah. It would be unfair of me to put the entire brunt of the blame on you, when it was my children who nearly managed to burn down the house and my life's work." He searched for words. "I — it means a lot to me, my work. I can't bear anyone to touch it. Least of all see it burned." One corner of his lip quirked upward.

"Is it all gone?" Miss Weston wrung her hands.

"No, it is salvageable. Most of it is still here. I will have to redraw some diagrams, however."

"I apologise, sir. You're right in that children always need supervision." She hung her head.

He cleared his throat. "Well. You are never to let them out of your sight from now on."

Her knuckles whitened as she clutched her satchel. "So you'd really like me to stay?" Her voice quivered.

Philip nodded. "If you please. My children will never forgive me if you leave. Just don't allow them to burn down the house again."

"Oh." Colour flooded her cheeks again. She sighed with relief.

"I will find a safer place for my work, far away from any fire." He piled his arms full of papers and books and went to the door. Arabella stepped aside to let him through. He nodded at her.

She gave a wobbly smile. "Thank you, sir," she whispered.

He gave a curt nod. Dash it if those enormous eyes of hers weren't welling up again. Dewdrops in a summer morn. Philip shook himself.

If his thoughts continued in this vein, he'd end up writing poetry instead of calculations.

CHAPTER 11

*a*rabella stayed up until past midnight writing down everything she remembered from the seminary. The schedule, curriculum, and materials they'd used in each of the four years she'd spent there. Using this as an inspiration, she drafted a different schedule for each child, for each had different needs. She'd drafted an entire lesson down to the minute. She'd never be caught unprepared from now on. It filled her with a sense of purpose that was strangely satisfying.

Arabella chewed on the tip of her quill. All of them needed regular breaks and walks outside in the fresh air. She wanted to incorporate outdoor lessons that involved what nature had to offer. Identifying trees, bushes, flowers, birds, collecting leaves, sketching them with pencil, coal, and watercolour. Her mind buzzed. They needed time for quiet reading, drawing, and individual work. The list of materials that she needed grew.

Arabella leaned back, rubbing her eyes. The candle had burned down to a flat blob of wax and would fizzle out soon. It was time for bed.

What a day it had been. Her heart had stopped when Mr Merivale had stormed into the parlour, wrath sparking out of his eyes when he saw her holding the burning parchment.

Had he thought she'd burned them on purpose? She'd felt humiliated when he dismissed her.

Then he'd changed his mind. He'd been right that it had been her responsibility to supervise the children at all times. Arabella vowed she'd never give him reason to reprimand her again.

Then she remembered that tomorrow was probably going to be a different story entirely.

For it was her turn to cook.

Arabella knew nothing about cooking. She'd never even seen their cook at Ashmore Hall actually cook. She somehow whisked culinary miracles out of thin air that not only tasted wondrously good, but that looked like works of art. Lobster Rissoles, Roast Quarter of Lamb, Charlotte Russe, Neopolitan cakes, Vol-au-vent of pears…. Her stomach grumbled.

"It can't be that difficult," she told herself before she dropped off to sleep.

ARABELLA GOT UP BEFORE EVERYONE ELSE AT DAWN. SHE slipped into the kitchen and stared at the iron stove with misgiving. The day Katy interviewed her had been the first time she had seen a real kitchen — from the inside. She had no idea what most contraptions were used for. She was a duke's daughter. She shouldn't be doing this. It didn't befit her station, her breeding, her sense of what was appropriate. Besides, she had no clue where to begin.

"I can do this," she muttered. People had been cooking since time immemorial. One needed a fire, and — something to cook with.

She looked around. First. Make a fire. That was all well and good, but how? She'd never had to make a fire in her entire life. Even at Miss Hilversham's Seminary they'd had a maid to do it for them. Everything had been done by servants. They'd dressed her, fed her, turned down the bed, pulled up her stockings, cleared out the chamber pot…

Arabella swallowed. That had been, so far, the most unpleasant act. Earlier, she'd taken her chamber pot outside and, holding her nose with two fingers, she'd poured it into what she hoped was the right place to deposit this stuff. Terrible, to think that one's job was to do this on a daily basis. Yet some servants had to do that.

But back to the business at hand. Fire. Cook.

How?

She saw an odd device lying on the mantlepiece and picked it up. It wasn't a tinderbox, which her maids used. A tinderbox was a small, round metal box that contained tinder and flint and somehow, if used correctly, it would produce a spark that created a fire. The device she held in her hands was different. There was no lid to take off, and it did not seem to contain any tinder, though — she peeked into a crack in the box — it did seem to contain flint. She held it in her hand, clueless. What was she supposed to do with it? Was this one of Mr Merivale's inventions? It seemed to have a spring. She pressed down on the sides and — it created a spark! Arabella nearly dropped it.

It took her several tries, and finally, she managed to light a candle with Mr Merivale's odd tinderbox.

When the fire finally burned in the stove, she stared at it, a feeling of awe suffusing her. She'd just made a fire!

Next, she would cook breakfast. Her eyes fell on the basket of eggs by the window.

An hour later, Philip and the children entered.

"Breakfast is ready." Strands of hair stuck to her sweaty

temples, and her shoulders hurt. She'd never felt so exhausted.

"Ah! Wonderful." Philip rubbed his hands and sat down. "I see you have made —" He stared at the yellow gob on his plate. "Kedgeree."

Arabella hoped it was edible. She'd wanted to make an omelette but had forgotten to add some grease to the pan. Once she'd figured out how to do it, she'd found the act of cracking eggs into the pan so oddly satisfying that she'd gotten carried away and added too many eggs, a dozen or so, with some shell as well. The mass quibbled in the pan, and she'd had no idea how to turn it into a uniform, smooth thin omelette like the cook at Ashmore Hall had produced. Watching the Merivales clean up their plates, she concluded they didn't seem to mind overly much.

Mr Merivale spooned some of the egg mass into his mouth. "Quite excellent," he said, then took a big gulp from his cup. "Pray, Miss Weston, are you in love?" he asked in a casual, jesting way after he set down his cup.

Arabella's cheeks burned. "Of course I'm not! Why would you say that?"

"You do know what they say about cooks who put too much salt into the food?" His lips quirked with amusement.

"I know no such thing. What are you talking about?"

"A lovelorn cook oversalts the soup." Mr Merivale grinned. "Who's the lucky fellow?"

"Never heard of this proverb." Arabella tugged at a strand of hair that had come loose. "It's nonsense. You must've made this up."

Her discomfiture seemed to amuse him. "It's a German proverb. The reason being when one is in love, one doesn't pay too much attention to the amount of salt one adds to the soup. One of my comrades, who had ties to Germany, liked to tease us with it when we spooned our soup from our tin cans. It's because our cook kept oversalting our food. Alas, he didn't make it through the war." He stared broodingly at nothing in particular.

Arabella noted that the light, teasing cheer dissipated quickly as a shadow fell across the table. She racked her brain.

"'Give neither advice nor salt, until you are asked for it,'" she finally shot back. "English proverb. It is most sensible." She was pleased with herself.

He quirked a smile at her. "Very proper and moralising, Miss Weston. I must say, I prefer to imagine you in love."

"Have you ever been in love, Miss Weston?" Katy asked.

All pairs of eyes were on her. Mr Merivale lifted his eyebrow in anticipation. She could not blush a deeper shade of red, and so she shrugged with a laugh.

"Of course I have." She spooned her eggs stoically. "Everyone falls in love eventually. It's part of the human condition."

"Is it?" Mr Merivale propped his head in his hand on the table and studied her with interest.

Katy's eyes brightened. "Oh, do they? Because I can't ever imagine falling in love. Ever. Not like Papa and Mama were in love."

Arabella threw him a curious look. Now it was Mr Merivale's turn to flush. He cleared his throat loudly. "How on earth did we end up talking about this?"

"You started it. We were talking about salt." Now it was Arabella's turn to enjoy his flustered demeanour.

"Very true," he muttered and shoved another forkful of eggs into his mouth.

"Or how about this one." Arabella began to enjoy herself. "Salt is good for the mind, the spirit, and gives one joy of life."

"That's a good one." He nodded appreciatively. "Haven't heard that one yet."

She grinned. "That's because I just made it up."

"Very well done, Miss Weston." He threw her an appreciative look that made her feel fuzzy inside.

"I like it." Robin dug enthusiastically into his eggs. "Salt and all. You should cook every day, Miss Weston."

"Heaven forbid," she shuddered. "Then we'll be eating oversalted eggs for breakfast, lunch, and dinner."

"I have to say, Miss Weston. I didn't think you'd had it in you," Mr Merivale admitted as he put the fork down.

"You liked it? You really did?" She felt the sun rise.

His eyes twinkled. "It wasn't the worst egg I've ever tasted. The other day, Katy managed to miraculously produce purple eggs." He chuckled.

"Purple eggs! How so?"

"I wanted something special. Not the same old omelette. So I added violets," Katy explained.

"I am sure it tasted wonderful," Arabella said. "You're a good cook."

"So are you." Katy replied with a big smile. "Your eggs are better than mine."

"Especially since they were prepared with gentle hands that previously never have had to cook." Mr Merivale leaned back in his chair, teasing laughter dancing in his eyes. "Or make fire?"

He couldn't have seen how she'd fumbled with the tinder box earlier?

"These hands are capable of so much more than just cooking," Arabella retorted, suddenly overcome with that old feeling again, that urge to prove that she wasn't entirely useless.

"I have no doubt about that," he said softly, looking at her hands that rested on the table. Her skin tingled. She rubbed the back of her hand with her thumb.

Philip got up. "Well. Back to work." He strode to the door and turned. "You are not any less talented for not knowing how to do some things, Miss Weston. I just wanted you to know that."

Arabella felt something warm spread in her chest. "Thank you, sir."

"Thank you for breakfast, Miss Weston," the children told her before they scampered out of the room.

Arabella felt a feeling she'd never felt before: the feeling of satisfaction when one produced food that was eaten.

CHAPTER 1 2

*M*iss Weston and the children had disappeared into the parlour, and Philip hadn't seen any of them since. He'd cleared out the parlour earlier, so they could use it as a school room.

Philip chuckled at the memory of breakfast and the over-salted eggs. She hadn't noticed, but he'd watched her through the kitchen window. She'd first stood in the kitchen, lost, then struggled with his improved tinderbox, as he called it, his very own invention. A laugh escaped him. She'd struggled with the fire, too, first putting in too many logs, then taking them all out again, then putting in too much paper, then taking it all out again as well, then alternating between logs and paper. She'd crouched on the floor, her hair undone, her cheeks red with blowing into the sparks. He'd expected her to give up and dissolve into tears. He was about to have mercy on her and relieve her of the task. Instead, he'd heard her utter an unladylike curse and growl, "I can do this, if it's the last thing I'll ever do." And then she did.

A feeling of grudging admiration took hold of him. She

wasn't one who gave up easily. She wasn't the milk-and-water miss he'd feared she'd be. This Miss Weston had gumption. She was a problem solver. Just like him.

Philip walked past the open door to the parlour with the pretext of obtaining a mug of ale from the kitchen. To his surprise, the children were sitting at the table, their heads bent over their slates. He hovered behind the door to listen.

"I am going to invent a flying machine," he heard Robin say. "It's going to look like this." He heard the chalk squeak on the slate.

Ah. Brilliant child.

"How clever of you, Robin," he heard Miss Weston say. "But now we want to focus on our Latin. Shall we? Translate 'the bird flies under the cloud'."

"*Avis volat in nube.*"

"Try again."

"*Avis volat sub nube.*"

"Almost. It's *avis volat sub nubem*," she corrected. "And now try to say, The bird flies through the cloud."

"My machine will definitely fly higher than any bird, Miss Weston, and far higher than any cloud."

"Excellent, Robin, then write it down in Latin."

"But I want to write 'my hydrogen-filled balloon flies to the moon,'" Robin announced. "What's hydrogen balloon in Latin?" She groped for words.

"How do you say ornithopter with flap–valve wings in Latin?" Robin pressed.

"I have to admit I don't know, Robin. The ancient Romans wouldn't have known the term, either."

Robin threw his stencil down. "Bah. Then what's the point of learning Latin? Nothing interesting existed for those old Romans. Useless language."

"Use the word 'machine' instead. *Machina.*"

"That's not the same at all," Robin argued. "A machina is too general. An ornithopter is a specific device. It flaps its wings like a bird." He flapped his elbows in imitation.

Miss Weston sighed.

"Here, I'll show you." Robin scrambled on top of the desk.

"Robin, sit down," Miss Weston said sharply.

"It flaps its wings like this," Robin flapped his arms, "and then it takes off — whoo!"

He jumped from the table and crash-landed on the floor. "Ow." "Robin, stop being silly! I can't concentrate," Katy complained.

"Robin, are you hurt?" Miss Weston bent over him.

"No." He rubbed his elbows.

"I am very cross with you." Miss Weston said it in such a sweet manner that Philip rolled his eyes.

"Sit down now and write your sentences. And you, Katy, after you have finished the passage on Cicero you may attempt to summarise it."

"I would love to have music lessons next, Miss Weston."

Philip grinned. Naturally, his Katy was dictating the curriculum.

"If we could, we would, Miss Katy. Unfortunately, there is no pianoforte in this house."

"All ladies know how to play the pianoforte, right, Miss Weston?" Katy sounded whiny.

"Many do, you are right. But back to Cicero. Joy, try to copy 'mus' onto your slate in nice, clear letters. It means mouse."

"Mouse!" Joy stuck out a tongue at the corner of her mouth as she scraped her chalk across the slate.

"But, Miss Weston, if we could somehow *obtain* a pianoforte…"

Philip left quietly. The woman was doing well. Even

though she wasn't entirely to be trusted on account of her mysterious background, there was no doubt that she was good for the children. Sure, they were running ramshackle over her, but that wasn't his problem. They were learning Latin. Mind you, Robin was right that this dead language was entirely useless, but it was required at University. He might as well learn it. As for the pianoforte...He grinned. He'd let the woman figure out that conundrum. He returned to his forge, whistling.

THE NEXT MORNING, PEGGY, THE HOUSEMAID, RETURNED. SHE was a buxom woman with chestnut brown hair severely tied back, stretching the skin of her temples. She didn't seem to be the kind who talked much, but there was a twinkle in her eye and a softening in her face when she greeted the children.

"Peggy!" Joy threw herself into her arms and began garbling about mouse and her new governess.

Arabella, who'd gotten up when the maid entered, smoothed her skirt.

Peggy looked Arabella up and down and narrowed her eyes. "Governess?" The silent look on her face as she crossed her arms clearly expressed she expected Arabella to put on airs. "Where you sleepin'?"

"In the little room by the stairs."

Peggy pursed her lips. "That good enough for you?"

Arabella wasn't used to being quizzed by servants. She tilted up her chin. "Oh, yes. I am quite comfortable there."

Peggy gave Arabella a hard stare. Then she nodded curtly. "Well then. Today's washing day. If you want fresh things get them to me."

Arabella softened. "I will. Thank you, Peggy."

An hour later, the smell of freshly baked bread suffused the house.

Arabella had to admit that cooking was something she would gladly let more experienced people do. She was getting rather tired of eating oversalted eggs and burned pancakes with blackberry jam.

The children seemed to agree and chatted about what wonderful things they'd get to eat for supper the next few days. Arabella rapped on the table. "Back to work, children. We were declining French verbs."

Days passed quickly when one was happy. Before Arabella knew, she'd settled into a comfortable routine. Most of the mornings and afternoons were spent teaching the children. She spent additional one-on-one time with Katy on lessons of grooming and deportment, which Katy soaked up eagerly. Robin had rebelled against it, declaring he'd "prefer to learn three hours of additional Latin than silly girl's stuff" and Joy, who was initially enthusiastic about joining the big girls, tended to nap off during that time.

In the evenings and oftentimes well into the night, Arabella planned lessons. She thought she got better at it with each day. The children were cooperative and eager learners, and it was encouraging seeing them improve. Joy could read, but she couldn't write. And Katy could calculate with a swiftness that her mind steamed, but she had trouble writing coherent essays.

All three had to work on their penmanship. It was a disaster. Not to mention their father's. Arabella had puzzled a good five minutes over a note Philip had left on the kitchen table one morning. She thought it read "Went to work. Proceed as usual." But it could also say "Don't work, process casually." The foundry outside where he usually worked had been oddly quiet, so she assumed it meant the latter, though it did not make much sense at all.

She saw surprisingly little of him these days. He often left before breakfast and returned in the evenings, which he spent alone with the children. Arabella wondered what he was doing during the day. On the rare occasion when they met in the hallway, he nodded at her and gave her a brief, tired smile. He was somewhat of a mystery, that Mr Merivale.

CHAPTER 13

As summer gradually ended, Arabella marvelled at the palette of colours that unfolded outside. The beaches glowed golden ochre, the water foamed white as it slapped against the brown cliffs, and the wind-swept moors turned a dusky rust red. She'd fallen in love with the wild Cornish landscape. The first time she saw the mist hover like silver lace over the dark cobalt blue ocean she exclaimed, "How picturesque it is! We need to buy watercolours so we can capture this beauty."

"But we don't have any watercolour paints, Miss Weston. And remember you promised we'd get some," Katy nagged. "We also need chalk, rulers, pencils, and a new chalkboard for Robin, because he broke it when he tried to turn it into a flying machine the other day."

"So he did." Arabella suppressed a smile, remembering the shattered fragments scattered on the floor. "Master Robin," she'd said sternly, imitating Miss Hilversham's tone. "Chalkboards can't fly. Even if you try to attach wooden wings and throw them down the stairs."

"Yes, Miss. It was just an experiment. I think the body

needs to be lighter and more flexible. I will try it again with lighter wings." Robin had scuttled off to set his plan into execution.

Arabella's mind whirled as she sat down to make a shopping list. The neighbouring farmer, Mr Argus, had offered to give them a ride to town in his cart. As the cart rumbled along the country road, they passed a marbled gate that led to a wide alley with oak trees. Behind it must be an estate of considerable size.

"Who lives there?" Arabella asked Katy.

"I don't know. Someone." She turned her face away.

"That's Thornton Hall." Mr Argus threw Katy an odd look. "Surely you know that?"

Katy shrugged. "Papa says we are not to put a foot there. Ever."

"Doesn't surprise me," Mr Argus muttered.

Katy's face darkened. "I went there once, with Mama. I never want to go there again. They look down on us and snub us horribly if we don't hold the teacup properly, or say the right things, or curtsy the right way. They think we're riffraff."

Arabella threw her a surprised look. "Riffraff!"

"We aren't genteel enough, I s'ppose." She lifted her chin. "Even if we were, we don't know how to behave properly. Papa says it doesn't matter and we should never care about what other people think and that we always ought to be proud of who we are. Even if we don't have much money."

Arabella looked at Katy and wondered what kind of woman her mother had been, and what they had experienced there. She did not want to press her further because Katy had clamped her lips shut, crossed her arms and turned away.

Mr Argus glanced sideways at Arabella. "It's an old story."

"What is?" Arabella threw him a puzzled look.

He opened his mouth to say something, then glanced at

the children and snapped it shut again. "I s'ppose it's not for me to say," he muttered. "Sorry, Miss. Best talk to Mr Merivale."

While Robin and Joy, leaning against each other, nodded off as the horses trotted slowly along the road, Arabella wondered what Mr Argus had been about to say.

The cart drove around a curve and the little harbour town appeared.

It was quaint with whitewashed cottages jumbled together and a main street with cobbled stone that had the most necessary shops. Mr Argus pulled the cart to a halt.

"Right. Here we are. You go about your business and I mine. We meet again in three hours?"

Arabella nodded and thanked him.

Katy pulled her towards a shop on the main street which seemed to burst with books, paper, quills and parchments. "There it is, Pethick's Books and Stationery."

It was the first time Arabella would be entering a shop like this. She usually frequented bigger fashionable shops on Bond Street in London. So it was with a considerable amount of curiosity that she pushed the door open to Pethick's Bookshop. It was a small place cramped with book-shelves. They not only had Joy's primer, but also a children's *Manners and Morals* book, as well as *Aesop's Fables*, which the little girl would enjoy. Especially the stories involving mice.

"You don't happen to know where to buy pianos here, do you?" Arabella asked the burly man behind the counter.

Pethick scratched his beard. "No ma'am, but I can help you order one from London if you need one. I'm only a bookseller but I get my goods straight from London, and I have my connections. Which kind do you want?"

Arabella thought of her gleaming grand piano at Ashmore Hall.

"A Broadwood. A grand piano. Six octaves."

The man's bushy eyebrows rose. "Broadwood, eh? Going for the best of the best, I see. That will cost," he pulled out his abacus and flicked the beads across the counting tablet, "roughly one hundred pounds if you buy it and half if you rent it. Plus transportation. Plus commission for me, yes?"

Arabella's face fell. "I had no idea it was so expensive. I'm afraid I can't afford it."

He nodded. "Aye, only the grandest families can afford to buy a Broadwood. You could rent one." He gave her a figure that was considerably less, but still beyond her means.

Arabella shook her head.

Pethick, however, seemed determined to be helpful. "If all things fail, you could rent the old pianoforte from Widow Woodhouse. She mentioned the other day she had no use for it anymore since she's lost her eyesight and that she would gladly give it away in return for a companion who'd read to her."

Arabella's face brightened. That seemed like an interesting proposition. "Widow Woodhouse, you said?"

"Aye. She lives in a side street not far from here." He explained to her how to reach her place.

"We want to wait outside in the sunshine, it's too damp and dark in here." Robin complained.

"Very well, but stay in front of the shop." Arabella replied, distracted. "I need a few more minutes. Katy, afterwards we can go visit Miss Woodhouse to see whether she'll rent us her piano. We can also visit the haberdashery and get some ribbons for the yellow dress."

Katy clapped her hands with delight. "Oh yes, let's do that!"

"Are ye Mr Merivale's wife?" Mr Pethick threw her a curious glance.

She felt a blush of red creep over her cheeks. "Oh no. I am just the governess."

"Governess, eh? Well, that explains it." A grin crept over his rugged face.

Arabella, in the process of pulling out her reticule to pay him, paused. "What do you mean?"

"Why he's been going from shop to shop and slaving since dawn. He's dragged loads of crates to the storage room for me. Then he went shovelling coal at Mornick's, and now he's lugging bags of flour for the baker." The man shook his head. "Never seen a man work so hard. Mind you, not that he needs to do it. But that's why we respect him. He's one of us. Down-to-earth, hard-working, and decent to the bone he is, that man."

Arabella looked at him, bewildered. "What are you talking about?"

The man shook his head. "Nothing. He said he'd do the ledgers for me, too. Forgot 'em here. Can I trust you to deliver the books to him?" He peered at her through narrowed eyes.

"Of course, I will put them safely into his hands." Arabella was dazed by what the man had told her.

Mr Pethick stepped to the window, stemmed his hands at the waist and shook his head. "He's right across the street."

Arabella couldn't make him out at first. There was a rugged worker in a sooty shirt with rolled up sleeves to reveal muscular upper arms, hauling a heavy sack of flour onto his shoulders and walking with slow, measured steps into the side entrance of the bakery.

"Look, there's Papa." Katy stood next to her and waved at him.

That was Mr Merivale? A jolt of surprise went through her.

He looked like an ordinary manual labourer, the kind she'd never brush sleeves with.

"Where are the other two?" Being thus preoccupied with

their father, she'd forgotten about Joy and Robin. She looked up and down the street and a rush of panic filled her when she did not immediately see them. Wasn't she supposed to supervise them every single second? How could that have slipped her mind so soon?

Hadn't she told the children to wait in front of the shop? She stepped out into the street, when Katy said, "They are over there," and pointed to the other end of the street. "They are talking to a man in the coach..."

A black, elegant carriage with a pair of white stallions stood at the end of the high road. A white-haired man talked to the children through the window. Something about this didn't seem quite right. Robin seemed frozen and Joy hid behind his back. Arabella rushed towards the carriage. The carriage door opened, and she saw a white, spindly hand beckon. She saw Robin hesitate —

"Robin!" Her shrill voice cut through the air. Robin's head jerked towards her, hesitated, then looked back at the old man. She stumbled over the cobblestone and nearly fell on her knees.

A roar came from behind her, followed by the sound of running footsteps, and a figure pushed past her.

"Don't you dare touch my children," Mr Merivale bellowed. He'd dropped the flour bags in the middle of the street and raced towards the carriage. "Robin, Joy. To me. Now!"

Robin stepped back, took Joy by the hand and turned towards his father.

Arabella reached the carriage, breathless, as the door closed. Merivale, his face red with rage, roared after the carriage. "Stay away from my children!"

As the carriage passed Arabella, she saw an old man lean back into its cushioned seats, with a sarcastic smirk on his face.

Arabella stopped and stared at the carriage as it pulled out of the town, disappearing around the curve.

Then she turned to Merivale, who hugged his children tightly. Katy came running and caught up with her.

"That was close." She gasped for breath.

"What happened just now?" Arabella asked her, but Katy bit her lip.

"Miss Weston." Arabella stepped back in surprise when she saw Mr Merivale's face contorted with rage. "You were supposed to supervise my children."

"I — well. Yes, of course, but we had to go buy some supplies —"

"For the second time you have left my children unsupervised, and it near ended in disaster. You are dismissed."

Again?

"I—" Arabella groped for words, then threw up her hands. "But I don't understand what happened!"

"Let us get one thing clear. My children are never, ever, under any circumstance, to talk to strangers. Especially not to sinister-looking ones who try to tempt them into their carriage. And you two — are you out of your minds?" Robin flinched. Joy's lips quivered, then she burst into tears. "How often do I have to tell you not to trust strangers and to get into their carriages!"

"He's not exactly a stranger," Katy muttered.

"Because he's tried this before, hasn't he?" Philip's voice shook.

Katy pressed her lips to a white line.

"But we didn't get into his carriage," Robin defended himself.

"No, but you were about to. What did he promise you this time? Sweets? Toys?"

"Kitten." Joy sniffled.

"He had a basket of little kittens inside." Robin looked

sullen. "He was going to give us one. He said we could choose one for each."

"Good God." Philip raked his hand through his hair. "An old man with kittens. And you should be old enough to know better. You want kittens? I can procure an entire litter, but never, ever get into a stranger's carriage. Robin, Joy. Is that clear?"

Robin blinked back his tears and nodded.

Philip exhaled shakily, then gathered Joy and Robin to him. "I am sorry I shouted at you," his voice was thick with emotion. "You gave me such a fright, my heart nearly jumped out of my body. I couldn't bear it if something ever happened to you."

"Nothing will happen to us, Papa," Robin mumbled into his shirt. "I can take care of us all."

Philip ruffled his head. "That's my boy." His voice wobbled. His eyes met Arabella's. She looked away and shifted from one foot to the other.

"Oy!" Mr Pethick, the grocer, came huffing towards her. "You forgot your things. The ledgers, and the shopping." He handed her two leather books and the wrapped-up parcel. "I gave the gal the ledgers, sir. I need 'em done by tomorrow."

"Certainly." Philip untangled himself from his children. "You all go home now with Miss Weston. I have some more work here left to do."

"So am I not dismissed?" Arabella asked timidly.

He gave her a hard look, turned and stalked back to his sack of flour.

She supposed that meant no.

She exhaled a shaky breath. "Before we go, children, I'd like to make one more visit."

Mrs Woodhouse's crinkled face broke into a delighted smile when she opened the door to Arabella and the three

Merivale children. "I never receive visitors, you see." She beamed and ushered them inside.

Mrs Woodhouse was more than willing to lend her piano to Katy, in return for weekly reading sessions with Arabella.

Mr Argus promised to pick up the piano for them later on in the day.

Arabella returned with the children to Rosethistle Cottage, satisfied, but also drained. Too many things had happened that day.

Philip arrived later in the evening, in time for supper. His face looked drawn and tired. He barely seemed to register the pianoforte that stood in the parlour room. "If you will excuse us, Miss Weston." He held the door to the parlour room. "I need to spend some time with my children. Alone." He set his chin and his demeanour was distant. He looked at her as if she were a stranger.

"Of course."

He nodded and closed the door.

Arabella stood in the dark hallway, her chest constricting. She heard their voices chattering through the closed door. Arabella went back and sat on her narrow bed.

For the first time, Philip had made her feel like she really was a governess, a domestic who worked for the family, but who didn't really belong with them and never would.

It was only natural, of course.

Then what was this dull yearning in her heart?

CHAPTER 14

*S*he was in the middle of recounting how Hannibal conquered the Alps, when someone hammered on the front door. Peggy couldn't open, because she was out washing laundry, and Mr Merivale was in town again, so the banging continued relentlessly.

Arabella looked around cluelessly, until she realised that the banging would continue because there were no servants who'd open the door.

Katy looked up from her work. "Do you want me to go see who it is, Miss?"

Arabella set down the book from which she'd been reading aloud. "No, finish writing your essay. I'll do it." She strode to the door and opened it.

A man wearing a dark blue livery with shiny brass buttons and a white, powdered wig snapped to attention. "I have a message for the earl, ma'am."

Arabella felt catapulted back to Ashmore Hall's blue drawing room, where footmen delivered messages like that. She gaped at him.

"Ma'am?"

"Did you say earl?"

He shuffled his feet. "Yes, Ma'am. The Earl of Threthewick, Ma'am?"

She shook her head. "There is no such person here. This is the residence of the Merivales."

The man wrinkled his forehead. "This is Rosethistle Cottage, Ma'am?"

"Yes, it is."

The footman looked unhappily at the missive that he held out to her. "I am to deliver this to Rosethistle Cottage for the Earl of Threthewick."

"Maybe there has been a mistake. This is the home of Mr Philip Merivale and his children Katy, Robin, and Joy. I am Miss Weston, the governess." A thought occurred to her. "Maybe you meant to deliver this to the big estate house that is nearby? Thornton Hall?"

He shook his head. "I'm from there." The footman scratched his head under the wig. "I'm new here. Is there another cottage called Rosethistle somewhere?"

"Actually, I don't know. I don't think so. It would be odd if there were two houses with the same name, wouldn't it?"

"Then this is the right place." He pressed a letter into her hands.

"But —"

"I'm sorry, Ma'am. I have to return. Dashed busy day today."

He scuttled off and left her staring at the letter in her hands. There was evidently a mix–up.

She left the missive on the side table in the hallway for Philip. He would have to decide what to do with it.

"Back to Hannibal," she announced brightly as she re-entered the parlour classroom. "Where were we? Hannibal marched into Italy with an army of war elephants —"

"He would've been a lot faster if he'd taken a balloon," Robin grumbled.

"I'm sure he would, Robin. As I was saying…"

Sometime later, Mr Merivale passed by the window outside, holding the letter. She was about to open the window to call out to him that it had been delivered by mistake, when she saw him break the seal and read it.

The words froze on Arabella's lips.

He crumpled the missive into a ball and threw it aside. He stalked by with a black scowl on his face.

"Miss? I finished my essay. Can we have a short rest?" Robin's voice tore her out of her thoughts.

"Yes." She unclenched her fists and took a deep breath to steady herself. It looked like Mr Merivale had some explaining to do.

HE SHOULD HAVE KNOWN BETTER THAN TO TRUST *HIM*.

Philip had known that for as long they were living here, he couldn't trust anyone, and he'd been right. His children couldn't take one step out of their garden without being accosted by *him*. A streak of hot fury flashed through Philip as he remembered the events in town.

They'd had an agreement. He had promised to leave them in peace for as long as they lived here. Philip should've known better, because at the first opportunity *he*'d broken that agreement. And sent a letter with an invitation, wanting to discuss things in a civilised manner. Over a cup of tea? Philip snorted. Over his dead body more likely.

Philip ferociously hammered on the metal, flattening it to a thin sheet. A final, furious bash of the hammer tore a hole in the sheet. Blast. Now he'd ruined it and had to start anew.

He sighed and slumped against the anvil.

It had been a mistake to settle in Cornwall.

He'd nearly gotten Robin. For one awful moment Philip had seen red. A violent, blood red that covered his vision and hurtled him straight back into the past. He'd rather be damned than let the past repeat itself.

But where else could they have gone to live? Back to Scotland? His grandfather's thatched cottage was comfortable for two, maximum three people, but five, including Granda? He couldn't house all of them. Besides, he no longer wanted to live from his grandfather's pockets. He could take care of his own family. Or so he thought. Philip threw the hammer down in frustration.

Several months ago, they'd lost the flat in London. Mr Fitz, the landlord, with whom he thought he'd had an amiable relationship for the fifteen years they'd lived there, insisted they move out. It had come out of the blue. He didn't give any particular reason other than, as landlord, he had the right to claim his flat whenever he wished. Mr Fitz threw them out on the street. Philip had thought of punching him in the face, except he wasn't a quarrelsome man and hated physical confrontation. The urgency with which the landlord wanted them gone was unusual. A nugget of suspicion festered in Philip. *He* could've had a hand in that. A bribe, maybe? The best of men had difficulty resisting a good chunk of money.

Philip couldn't find another abode in such a short time. They could've stayed with friends, or he could have asked his in-laws, but Philip was too proud for that. Besides, he was estranged from them now. And to separate himself from his children? Never.

Then he'd received a letter from *him*, offering him Rosethistle Cottage. Philip hadn't been surprised, because he knew he had his spies everywhere. He must've known that Philip had lost the place and that he was desperately looking for something else. The only reason why Philip hadn't rejected Rosethistle Cottage out of hand was because it already belonged to him.

He'd just forgotten about it.

Rosethistle Cottage was where he'd spent the happier part of his childhood. It had been his father's, and he'd loved it here. The country air was better for the children than the smog and dirt in London. Where he invented did not signify, whether in Cornwall or in London, the patent office wouldn't work any faster for that.

It had seemed such a perfect solution. So he'd decided to pack up and come here. On the condition that *he* left them in peace. Which he did. Until now.

Philip wiped the sweat from his forehead.

Things had gone so well here. Even a governess had shown up on his doorstep. Unless, of course, she had been sent by *him*. Philip frowned as the familiar feelings of mistrust and doubt assailed him again. But he'd cross-examined Katy, and she'd sworn that she'd posted that ad, and it was something so like her to do. And Miss Weston really must have seen that ad in the paper. He'd seen the clip himself. No, Miss Weston had appeared out of her own volition. A governess with an upbringing that was uncomfortably genteel for his own taste. But blast it, governesses were supposed to have genteel backgrounds, weren't they? So what was the problem?

He picked up the poker and stirred moodily in the ashes.

The problem was he liked her far too well for his own peace of mind.

Philip nearly dropped the poker. He didn't just think that, did he?

One didn't like governesses. They were starchy, strait-laced creatures who always moralised. That's what he'd expected them to be. Mind you, he'd never really known any governesses, because he'd always been taught by men. He himself had attended a grammar school in London for only a short time and was tutored by the local rector when they lived in Scotland, who then helped him obtain a scholarship for Edinburgh University.

Miss Weston was neither starchy, straitlaced, nor did she moralise.

Her cooking was hideous, but what governess was expected to cook?

She was gentle and sweet in a way that his wife Jenny never had been. And proud. Oh yes, very proud.

Except she hadn't been proud when he'd thrown the door shut in her face the other night, and he'd seen the flash of hurt in her cornflower-blue eyes. He'd wanted to tear the door open again and apologise and gather her to him tightly and maybe press a kiss on those eyelids...

He dropped the poker. By George. He had not just thought about kissing the governess!

That was just perverse. He was turning into the kind of person he despised the most, the almighty employer who manhandled his female servants.

Maybe it was in the blood. Maybe he'd inherited precisely that tendency.

Horror flushed through him. He'd never, ever lay a finger on her. Not for as long as she was working for him.

Philip wasn't like *him.*

He felt an urge to see her. To check whether her eyes really were as blue as he remembered.

He went to the cottage and stood in the doorway, thunderstruck, as he took in the scene unfolding in front of him.

There was a piano in his parlour. A sleek, black Broadwood.

Katy, with her tongue sticking out of the corner of her mouth, was attempting to play the tune of a simple minuet, while Robin sat at the table with his fingers in his ears. Miss

Weston stood over Katy and pointed at the notes on the sheets in front of her.

Katy threw up her hands. "Show me again, Miss Weston."

She sat down next to Katy and played the simple Mozart melody with a sweet fluidity that made Philip catch his breath. It had been so long since he had heard music in his house.

"Mouse likes that music," Joy proclaimed.

"Where the blazes did you get the piano?" Philip winced at his own tone. It came out harsher than he'd intended.

The children looked up, surprised, and Miss Weston, blast her, looked at him with that adorably confused look on her face that she sometimes had when he did something unusual.

Katy jumped up. "Isn't it a beauty? Miss Weston organised it for us, and Mr Argus brought it from town in his cart. It didn't cost us a penny. Widow Woodhouse lent it to us in return for us visiting her. Didn't you notice it standing here since yesterday?"

Philip had to admit that he hadn't.

"I know I should've asked your permission first. But things developed rather faster than anticipated." Arabella looked apologetic.

He shook his head. "You are a miracle, Miss Weston. I was only joking the other day when I told you to procure a piano."

"Yes, well, it isn't entirely free. I shall have to spend every Friday afternoon with the Widow. Will that be acceptable to you?"

She tucked a strand of blonde hair that had escaped from a bun that seemed like it didn't hold very well. If he untucked that pin that half-peeked out from her hair, would it tumble down to her waist, or lower?

"Mr Merivale?"

"Play something." He waved his hand. "Something proper."

Arabella hesitated. "Very well." She sat down, spread her fingers over the keys and closed her eyes. Philip sat down next to Joy on the sofa.

Then she played. By Jove. How she played. He did not know much about music, but even his unschooled ears could recognise music of quality when he heard it. It must be Beethoven, or Mozart, or something of the sort. It was deeply powerful. Her slim fingers danced over the keys, and he saw the little golden hairs curl in her graceful, swanlike neck as she bent over the piano, with eyes half-closed. When was it the last time he'd heard such magic? Powerful feelings surged in him. He swallowed.

Then she came to an end, and the children clapped, delighted.

"I want to be able to play like you, Miss Weston," Katy proclaimed.

Philip cleared his throat. "That was well done," he said gruffly. She was a bloody miracle.

A faint pink sheen spread over her cheeks. "Thank you. But we ought to continue with our classes now. Unless there was something particular that you wanted?"

Yes. Why had he come here again? He could hardly remember.

"Have you come to teach us arithmetic, Papa? Miss Weston's problems are easy as pie." Robin yawned to underscore his point.

"Another time. I wanted to ask whether —" Blast it, what was he that he wanted to say? He scratched his neck. "Have you all eaten properly?" he blurted out. He'd been sitting with them at the same table an hour ago, and he knew very well they'd all stuffed themselves with Peggy's roast chicken.

"Yes, Mr Merivale. Dinner was very good." She kept

looking at him, and his heart started to beat away in an unusual fashion.

"No burned pancake with blueberry jam for a change." He grinned to play over his awkwardness.

"No." She set her jaw. "If there's nothing else, I hope you won't mind if we continue our lessons?"

"Lake," he blurted out. Blast it if he didn't feel like a schoolboy himself. "Let's go to the lake," he clarified, almost sighing with relief when he saw their faces brighten.

The children dropped their studies and rushed outside.

"There's a small lake nearby that is perfect for swimming with children. It's warmer than the ocean," Philip explained.

When the sound of rushing footsteps abated, Miss Weston said with a frown, "Mr Merivale, this won't do at all." Now she did look all starchy and governess-like.

"You can continue your studies later. No one can think in this heat, and the children need to cool down." It wasn't that warm outside, but it was tolerably sunny, and the water would be bloody cold.

"Very well." She set the book down. "They did have trouble concentrating today."

"You're not coming?"

She shook her head.

"I need help supervising the children," he heard himself say.

Her shoulders relax as she relented. Finally. "Very well, sir," she said but kept her eyes averted. He wondered why.

PHILIP THREW SIDELONG GLANCES AT HER AS THEY WALKED down the path to the lake. Her face was shaded by the straw bonnet, and he couldn't see her expression. "When you were a child, what was your favourite past time?" Philip asked the first thing that popped into his mind, just to get her to speak.

She looked up, startled. "Favourite past time?"

"Yes. You know. Like horse riding, maybe? Swimming?" He opened the gate that led over the meadow. The lake was beyond. "What do you do for fun?"

"Fun," she said slowly. "There was no fun when I was little. The word wasn't uttered at all. I read, played piano, and embroidered. The height of the day's excitement was a walk in the park."

Philip pulled a face. "So you never fished in a brook? Climbed an apple tree? Built a treehouse? Ran in the streets with a gang of other children?"

Arabella looked at him with big eyes and shook her head. "I grew up alone. Chaperoned by maids. My parents died early. One of my brothers as well." She shrugged. "I was raised by my older brother and my grandmother. There wasn't much time for fun."

"Hm. Sounds like you didn't have a very thrilling childhood. You also seem to have been an extraordinary obedient child." He felt sorry for her.

"I'm very dull, am I not?" She sounded wistful. She thought for one moment, then her face brightened. "But I did run away, once. It was a rainy day, and I was keen on reading a book that was forbidden."

"Oho, a forbidden book! What was it?"

"It was a series of love poems." Arabella blushed. "My governess had expressly forbidden me to read them. Of course I had to read them."

"Aha, so there is hope. She disobeyed the governess! The skies shook and the world ended at such blatant disobedience?"

"Very nearly so. I snuck up into the attic, made myself a hideaway under a blanket, and read. The entire house was in a frenzy searching for me. I emerged four hours later, dusty, starving, and rather happy." She grinned at him. "I was punished severely. I had to sit in the schoolroom and copy the entire *Blessings of Morality* in one afternoon. It was dreadfully dull."

"May I ask what kind of forbidden work you read?"

"Lord Byron."

"Oho! The mad, bad, dangerous to know fellow?"

"Oh, yes. I adore Byron. Have you read his works?"

"No. I only read numbers. Tell me about it. What are your favourite lines?"

"She walks in beauty, like the night/ of cloudless climes and starry skies…"

He watched her, transfixed. Her face softened; a light glow entered her eyes. "It is like I can see her. Feel her, right there with him."

"You are right," Philip had difficulty tearing his eyes away from her face. An inner light lit up her eyes. She was beautiful. "You are not only musical, but you also have a deep sense for beauty."

"You have been on the continent, haven't you?"

Philip didn't reply for one moment. Then he threw the leaf away that he'd pulled from a tree. "Hm. Yes."

"Where?"

"Portugal. Spain. Belgium."

"What was it like at the peninsula? I mean, not the war. War must be the same everywhere. But the countries. Was Spain as hot as they say it is? Does the air flicker in the summer heat?" He thought for one moment.

Then he told her about Salamanca, the Arapiles, the barren landscape, and the city itself, with its incredible architecture, one of Europe's oldest Cathedral and University. "Not that we had much time to do sightseeing. We were too busy slaughtering and getting slaughtered."

Arabella drank in his words. "Salamanca. Where Columbus and Cervantes studied."

He looked at her, surprised. "Why, yes."

"I spent my afternoons alone in the library, reading. Not only Byron. But also newspapers and travelogues. I love travelogues especially. Stories of exotic countries I'll never get to see myself. India. China. Egypt."

"So not the quiet, docile girl after all. You secretly thirst for adventure. You are an armchair traveller."

She chuckled. "I have always envied those who were able to travel. One day, I will."

THE LAKE WAS A PICTURESQUE DOT OF BLUE FRAMED BY birches and weeping willows on its banks. The clear water lapped onto a pebbled little strip where the children had gathered. They arrived in time to see Robin throw himself headlong into the water. Katy helped Joy pull off her boots and dress, then both followed Robin in their petticoats. They squealed when their feet touched the cold water.

"My children are water creatures." Mr Merivale chuckled. "God knows where they got that from. We Merivales can't resist water."

"I once nearly drowned in a wishing well," Arabella confessed with a laugh.

His eyebrows shot up in surprise. "Wishing well? How so?"

"At Miss Hilversham's Seminary for Young Ladies. We went out on a midnight excursion to our neighbour's garden, which had a Celtic well. I made a wish for us all. Arrogant of me, I know. My friend Pen thought so, too. She disagreed with my wish and wanted to undo it. She insisted on retrieving the coin from the well and fell in. I tried to grab her, but she pulled me down."

"There were two of you in the well? You could've drowned!" His face went grim.

"Possibly. But I held on to Pen, who could swim." She shaded her eyes as she looked over the lake, watching the children splash about in the shallow water. "Lucy ran for help. So you see, nothing much happened." Other than her brother getting quite furious and pulling her out of her beloved school and getting her friend Lucy expelled. But that was a different story.

An easy smile tugged at the corner of his mouth. "As dangerous as it was, it must've been a sight."

Arabella's laughter rang out as light, clear peals.

"It sounds like you loved your time at the school," Philip observed.

"I did, oh, I did." Her voice grew wistful. "I wish I could've stayed, but my brother…"

"What happened? Why didn't you —" He waved a hand. "You know. Go to London, balls, get married. Whatever it is they do, those ladies."

She looked over the lake, the blue of the water mirroring her eyes. "I had my seasons. It didn't work." She picked apart a flower. She'd had three seasons and a fair share of marriage proposals, all of which she'd declined. None of the men had appealed to her. None of them saw her as something more than a duke's daughter. The only man with whom she'd imagined herself in love, a certain Mr Gabriel, had been oblivious to her feelings and married someone else. She'd felt a pang, but then moved on with her life. Was she as superficial as the rest?

He frowned. "This just confirms what I've been thinking all along. They are all idiots." He curled his lips in distaste.

She looked startled. "Who?"

"Society."

"Well, that's the way it is. There are certain rules in the beau monde. A girl has one season, maybe two. If she doesn't take…" she shrugged. "She'll end up on the shelf. A spinster."

Philip curled his lips. "The beau monde. Bah. There is nothing 'beau' about it. They're decadent, selfish, and cruel. Especially dukes. A more corrupt and degenerate lot doesn't exist. I despise them all wholeheartedly."

She looked at him with a slightly open mouth and widened eyes.

"You wouldn't want to marry one of those fellows anyway," he informed her. "No, Miss Weston. You're better off this way."

She snapped her mouth shut. "You are absolutely right." She swallowed.

"I would never want to marry a duke."

"To continue. What then?"

"My family — fell on hard times. We couldn't afford a third season." She bit her lip. "I didn't want to be a burden on my brother, so I answered Katy's advertisement."

Her face was smooth and serene. Almost too smooth.

He opened his mouth to prompt her further, when she hastily changed the topic. "Oh look, Joy really can swim."

He shaded his eyes. "Of course she can. I taught her myself. Joy, no doggy-swimming!" he called out. "Sometimes she does her hand movements like this," he rowed his hands in front of him, "When it should be like this." He spread his arms out wide. "But if you do this," he imitated the other movement again, "then sooner or later you will go under. I've taught quite a few of my comrades to swim. Before Waterloo. I've been thinking of inventing a swimming device that works properly, that would be safe for children and for people who are not capable of swimming. I've had some ideas. But alas, the material," he shook his head. "It requires the use of a kind of fibre that floats naturally on water. I have not yet found that material."

"Mr Merivale. I need to ask you something." She fixed a pair of anxious eyes on him.

"Anything," He said. Then cleared his throat. "I mean, supposing it is within a reasonable frame."

"Do you think you could teach me how to swim?" Her eyes were earnest as they met his. Something stirred deeply inside him. He was moved by the whimsical nature of the request.

"Of course, Miss Weston. Any time." He heard himself say. "When would you like to start?"

"If you don't mind. Immediately."

CHAPTER 15

*S*he would have to take off her dress. It was highly improper for her employer to see her in her petticoat. She scuffed the toe of her boot in the pebbled sand.

Arabella wrestled with herself for only a moment. Then she made a monumental decision. She could continue being the old Arabella, bred as the duke's daughter, full of stiff propriety. Or she could throw it all out and embrace the freedom that came with casting aside her old self. She decided that she no longer wanted to have anything to do with the old Arabella.

She stepped under the branches of a weeping willow and pulled off her dress. She hung it over a branch and emerged, with flaming cheeks, in her petticoat.

Philip, however—she'd begun to think of him as Philip, no longer as Mr Merivale—neither seemed to care nor notice what she was wearing. For that she was grateful. He took off his jacket.

And then he'd pulled off his shirt. Arabella almost fanned herself. It was the second time she saw him without a top.

For a moment it looked like he was about to take off his

pants, too, but then he didn't. Thankfully. Or regretfully. Arabella wasn't sure which one. She now understood why it was considered highly indecent for men to take off their shirts. Interesting how he was so entirely unaware that it was a breach of etiquette of the highest proportion. He'd always blithely ignored all rules of propriety, it was part of who he was. A man never took off items of clothing in the presence of a lady. It was unthinkable.

Then he taught her how to swim.

In her petticoats.

"You can do this, Miss Weston," he'd said cheerfully, as he moved further and further away from her and she scrambled to reach him. "Remember the arm movements." It wasn't easy attempting to swim when her petticoats clung to her legs. He was a hard teacher. With him, there were no gentle introductions. He'd led her to the deepest part of the lake, and it was literally, swim or drown.

And then, miraculously, she did it.

She swam.

Katy, Robin, and Joy swam next to her, cheering her on.

She could swim! She could really, truly swi—

And then her foot got tangled up in some seaweed, and she sank under water.

Philip pulled her out, and the odious man was laughing as she spluttered. "Good job, Miss Weston. Good job."

He helped her to the shore. His warm hand on her arm lingered, and it tingled all the way to her toes. He'd opened his lips to say something, but they just remained half open.

She noticed he not only had brilliant eyes but also full, sensitive lips. She couldn't tear her gaze away.

Then he blinked, cleared his throat, dropped his hands, and turned away.

"Let's make a fire. I told Peggy to bring towels and a basket with some things to eat."

She changed back to her dry dress and left her wet petticoat hanging on a branch to dry. When she emerged from behind the tree, she saw Peggy arranging a blanket on the ground and setting out plates with fruit and cheese. Arabella's stomach growled.

Philip and Robin built a fire. Katy handed her a stick. "We're having stick bread for dinner," she explained.

They twisted globs of dough around sticks and roasted them over the open fire, turning the sticks slowly until the bread turned brown and crusty, while remaining fluffy inside. The smell of wood, smoke, and freshly baked bread suffused the air.

"Don't hold it directly into the fire, or else it'll burn," Philip warned, as he helped Joy turn her stick. "Next time use less dough, then it bakes faster."

"But I'm so hungry, Papa." Joy licked her lips in anticipation.

Arabella picked the crispy crust off the stick with her fingers and popped it into her mouth. She closed her eyes. She'd never eaten anything so good.

They gathered around the fire, the Merivales, huddled in their towels, with strands of wet hair plastered to their faces, munching with open mouths, while talking at the same time. Robin explained his flying machine, which he wanted to get patented. Philip listened and nodded.

He didn't brush him off or tell him it was impossible. He was taking his children's flights of fancy seriously.

The orange golden flames flickered over Philip's face as he talked, animated, using both his hands to explain.

"Robin is onto something great, here. I know it is difficult to believe, Miss Weston, but one day we will be able to invent machines of such perfection, anything will be possible. We'll be able to fly."

Arabella, in a dream-like state, looked up, saw the stars twinkle down on her. "Even to the moon?"

He leaned on his elbow and lifted his face. "Certainly. To the moon. And beyond."

"In a flying machine." Robin sighed. "I wish I could be in it."

"Me too," she heard herself say. "I'd join you in a jiffy."

Philip, his hair sticking out in all directions, turned to her with a smile so boyishly happy her heart stopped. Only to resume a moment later, hammering away in a rhythm that was alarming. She pressed her hand over it, afraid the others would hear it.

A feeling of golden honey warmth flooded through her body.

That night, Arabella couldn't sleep. Her mind was a heated jumble of the day's events. She'd been living with the Merivales for six weeks. Not a day had gone by that hadn't been eventful. But today had been quite different. It had been magical.

It had been so easy, so natural to talk to him. He'd listened as if he'd been truly interested in what she had to say. There'd been admiration in his eyes. And humour. When he laughed, they turned a shade greener. But in the house or in the shadow, they took on a greyish hue.

How easy it was to love them, she thought as she looked at the rays of moonlight that made silvery crinkles on her bedsheet. How easy it was to love him.

She sat up straight in bed.

Love?

She fell back and stared with a dry mouth at the ceiling.

Oh, no, no no no.

Oh yes, whispered her heart.

Oh yes.

CHAPTER 16

The next day was Arabella's day off and she welcomed it. She needed to get away from the Merivales, their energy, ideas, chaos, and charm. Her mind was too heated and jumbled. She needed to escape that constant sizzling feeling between her and Philip. She rubbed the goosebumps on her arms. Could one be hot and cold at the same time? If so, that was how Philip Merivale made her feel.

She hurried across the meadow behind the cottage, without any particular destination in mind. Her steps slowed when she reached the gate where the children had said they shouldn't enter. The place where Katy said the people considered them riffraff.

Overcome with curiosity, she stepped into the entrance drive and walked up the avenue lined with chestnut trees.

After a few minutes of vigorous walking, the trees cleared and a mansion appeared. Thornton Hall. It didn't exhibit the same kind of neoclassical pomp as Ashmore Hall, but it was sufficiently impressive. With turrets and towers of grey stone, it looked gothic and gloomy. The surrounding park was meticulously tended but had a soulless, deserted feeling, as if people had not been promenading there for a long time.

Arabella knew that it was common for housekeepers to give random guests a tour of the house if they asked for it. She decided that she would do precisely that.

The butler, who opened the door, looked as high in the instep as the butler at Ashmore Hall. Oh, but she knew how to deal with people like that. She'd done so her entire life. Arabella put on a sweet but slightly condescending smile.

"I would like a tour about the house."

He swept her with a glance. "We do not give tours to strangers." The butler made a motion to close the door in her face.

"Let her in," a voice said behind him.

"Yes, Your Grace."

Arabella looked curiously behind the butler, but since she stood in the sun and it was dark inside, she could only see a shadowy figure hovering in the back.

The door closed behind her, and it felt like the shadows swallowed her.

She shivered. She found herself in a vast marble hall. At the bottom of the stairs, next to a tremendous urn, stood a spindly-looking man, clutching a cane.

"I am the Duke of Morley," he said in a strong, rusty voice. "And you, I gather, are the Merivale's governess. Welcome to my home."

Arabella gasped when she recognised him.

He was the man in the coach.

Morley. It was the name Philip had uttered that day of the storm. He'd wanted to know whether Morley had sent her.

He wouldn't be pleased at all to know she was here.

"Maybe I should go," she mumbled and took a step back.

"Ring for Mrs Stanyon," the duke told the butler. "If you would like to see the house, you will do so." He waved about a bony hand to indicate the marbled splendour that surrounded them. It was like a tomb. "Miss — Forgive me, but I did not catch your name."

"Arabella Astley." She nearly bit her tongue the moment she uttered her real name. "Weston," she tagged on hastily. "Arabella Astley Weston." That wasn't well done. But the duke merely looked at her politely, giving no indication that he'd recognised the name Astley.

"Miss Weston."

Arabella nodded hard. "I really think I ought to go."

"Mrs Stanyon is my housekeeper, and she will give you a tour. I would like to give you the tour myself, but"—he knocked his stick against his legs —"these no longer cooperate as they ought to." He shook his head. "All these stairs."

Arabella didn't know what to think. He seemed a feeble old man, but there was a crafty look in his eyes that she did not like very much.

"Did you really intend to kidnap the Merivale children?" she blurted out. Then she clasped a hand over her mouth. She couldn't believe she'd just said that.

He cackled a laugh that did not sound amused. A woman appeared as if grown out of the ground.

"Ah, Mrs Stanyon. This lady here would like a tour. Take her to the gallery. We will meet for tea in an hour."

Alarm shot through her. She did not want to have tea with him later. But here was a chance to discover what was really going on. Arabella hesitated.

Mrs Stanyon held a set of keys in her hand that chinked together. "Very well, Your Grace." She threw a sharp look at Arabella. "If you would follow me, Miss."

Confused, Arabella followed the woman, who promptly began to rattle off a series of names and dates. "You must know that the name of Morley reaches back all the way to the Middle Ages and is traced back to William the Conqueror..."

After an hour of walking, Arabella's feet hurt. Most of the mansion, except for the duke's personal rooms, which they did not visit, was in disuse. The furniture was draped by holland covers. The curtains were drawn, and an eerie gloom had settled over the entire place. It smelled of dust and mildew. On the wall hung collections of paintings that rivalled Ashmore Hall's. The Morley family line was at least as old as her own. Yet, until she came to Cornwall, she'd never heard of the name.

"Finally, the gallery. If you would follow me, Miss." Mrs Stanyon strode ahead, while Arabella trailed after her.

The gallery was the only bright room in the entire house. Long and narrow, it was like a corridor, with a row of windows on one side, while the portraits hung on the other.

"This is Morley, the first duke who came over with William. He was known for his prowess in battle..."

Arabella's eyes glazed over. She couldn't care less about all those dour looking men with pointy beards and ugly wigs. There were only men hanging on the wall, not a single woman. She wrinkled her forehead.

"This is the current duke, the twenty-fifth Duke of Morley." They stopped in front of a life-sized portrait of the spindly-looking man who'd greeted her earlier. He was younger in the portrait since his hair was dark, whereas now it was entirely white. But he wore the same ill-pleased expression that all the other men wore.

Next to him hung the portrait of a more pleasant-looking young man with watery eyes and a slightly vapid, but dissipated expression. The housekeeper did not comment and passed him by. Next to it was a grey space where a portrait must have once hung.

"It is being restored," Mrs Stanyon explained. "And this one, here, is the Earl of Threthewick."

Arabella gasped.

For the charming smirk that greeted her was none other than Philip Merivale's.

CHAPTER 1 7

"I don't understand." Arabella clasped and unclasped her hands. "This makes little sense." After the gallery, Mrs Stanyon had taken her to a salon, where the duke was waiting for her in a fauteuil, a blanket covering his legs.

"First, some tea." The old duke lifted a finger, and Mrs Stanyon brought them cups of tea and a plate of biscuits. "To fortify your mind. It must have been a shock."

Indeed. Arabella had never fainted in her life, but when she met Philip's jade-green eyes in the portrait, she'd almost toppled to the ground.

"I cannot begin to tell you how morose and difficult my life has been. When my own flesh and blood denies me, when my plans are thwarted, leaving a bleak and lonely future, only death to look forward to. But now I see Fortuna's wheel is finally turning in my favour. What a joy it is to have you here, Lady Arabella."

She nearly sprayed a mouthful of tea across the tea table. Arabella spluttered an answer. Mrs Stanyon handed her a damask napkin. She covered her mouth.

A gleam of enjoyment lit up his grey face. That crafty old man. He'd known who she was all along.

"Oh, yes, Lady Arabella. Did you think I'd not recognise your name? You are the sister of the Duke of Ashmore. One of the most powerful men in the country." He looked pleased. "Why are you parading about as a governess in my grandson's employ?"

"Because I was bored with my life. I want to work." She'd blurted it out without thinking. She wanted to prove herself useful in life, that she could be more than just an ornament in a drawing room, but she wasn't about to say that.

"What nonsense. Work! I've never heard such a thing in my entire life. What does your esteemed brother say to that, I wonder?"

Arabella looked at him, alarmed. He raised his bony hand to appease her. "Never worry. Your secret is safe with me. But you must know you cannot hide quality in a pile of manure. Your lineage is everywhere, in your entire being. The way you move your head — yes, like this, precisely — the way you curl your lips in disdain. How you speak and pronounce your 'r's. It is in your blood. You can't hide it or deny it no matter how hard you try. Quality and breeding, down to the marrow. I approve." He clucked his tongue. "This is the lesson my boy refuses to learn. He tries so hard." He shook his head.

"Tries so hard to do what?"

"To be a commoner," he said mournfully. "A lower-class rat of the gutter."

Arabella drew her brows. "You shouldn't say that."

"Ah, but it is true." He took a slurpy sip of his tea and pulled his lips into a line of disgust. "Mrs Stanyon, how long have you worked here?"

"Nearly twenty-three years, Your Grace."

"Twenty-three years and you still don't know how to

116

prepare my tea?" He set down his cup with a clatter. "It is a hideous brew. It needs more sugar."

"Yes, Your Grace. But you know what the doctor says —"

"Balderdash. I want my tea as usual, or you are dismissed."

Mrs Stanyon handed him a second cup. "This time it has the right amount of sugar. But it is poison for your heart, says the doctor."

"Let an old man have his tea the way he enjoys it. Heaven knows there is such little enjoyment left in this miserable life of mine." He spilt half of the content with his shaky hands as he drank, then leaned back in his chair, satisfied. "Aah. Precisely as I have been drinking it these past seventy-six years of my life." He turned to Arabella. "I started drinking tea when I was four."

That meant he was—

"I am eighty." A bitter smile crossed his face. "I have had a long life, Lady Arabella. I have never lacked in anything. My marriage was arranged. It was loveless, but then, one does not expect to marry for love, does one? The duchess did her duty and promptly gave birth to two strapping boys. Twins. She conveniently died three years ago."

Arabella gasped.

"Are you shocked? It is the truth. It is better this way. We made each other's lives miserable."

"Still, to speak of someone like this…"

"It is neither here nor there. She is dead and gone, and that is all there is to it." What a horrid old man he was.

"But my boys, ah." His voice softened.

"The twins?"

"Edward and George." He pressed a spindly hand over his heart. "George was the oldest. He was to become the next duke." He closed his eyes as he talked. "Both were such lively, bright, intelligent boys. Disobedient and contrary to the bone. Devil's spawn, full of nonsense and mischief, cosseted by an overindulging mother." He opened his eyes. "I tried to beat it out of them but only achieved the opposite." There was a long pause as the old man stared off into nothing.

"Yes? So George was the heir," Arabella prompted. She'd forgotten her tea as she listened breathlessly.

"The stupid boy ran away to the war. One of those useless French revolutionary wars and promptly got himself killed." The duke shook his head as if he still did not believe it. "And Edward. He went and married a laundry maid." He moaned as if that pained him physically.

"Wait. Are we talking about Philip's father?"

"Yes. Philip's mother was a common rat in the gutter." He almost threw down the second cup of tea, and it splashed on the tablecloth.

"Well, let's just say he married beneath his station?"

The duke ground his teeth. "It was a mésalliance of the highest order. He did it only to spite me. I nearly disinherited him. But I have forgiven him because the union brought forth Philip." His entire face lit up. "He's been the sun in my life."

When the old man smiled, Arabella could see how handsome he must have been once. She could also see the family resemblance. He had the same high cheekbones and forehead as Philip.

Arabella shook her head. She still couldn't believe it. "So Philip's mother is a commoner. What happened to them?"

"Edward died in an accident when the boy was seven. The gutter rat raised him and instilled in him working-class ethics, as well as a pronounced fear of me." He sighed. "I am a wealthy man. So is Philip. He could be swimming in money. Instead, he prefers to be a blacksmith and tinker about with those —" He gestured with his hands. "Inventions. Bah. Yes, I know about those inventions. I have some influence in the patent office." He revealed his yellow teeth as he grinned. Turning to Mrs Stanyon, he said, "Bring the box."

She returned with a mahogany box and set it on his lap. It was filled with documents, designs, letters. Philip's inventions. She recognised his sloppy handwriting.

"I have bought them all. He doesn't know it, of course. He thinks the patent office has bought them."

"But — but—"

"He thinks he's been maintaining his livelihood with his own brain juice." He cackled a laugh. "The reality is he is living off the money of his grandfather, after all."

Good Heavens. And here was Philip, thinking he had his inventions patented in an orderly fashion. Arabella jumped up.

"Sit down, Lady Arabella. It is but a little gratification for someone, a little something for me to know I have something to give to my grandson after all. Would you begrudge me that?"

"But not like this! He believes the patent office has granted him a patent!"

"Not the most ethical thing to do, I agree. But then, I am not an ethical man. I am, apparently, the consummation of everything that is evil." He closed his eyes again. "Maybe he is right. Which accounts for why he wants nothing to do with me. It is impossible to erase that way of thinking once it has taken hold. He despises me for what I am. A duke."

It was true, Philip was uncommonly proud of who he was. He loathed the upper classes.

"And now?"

Morley sighed. "Now, Philip has three wonderful children. Their mother used to bring them here once, twice maybe. But that was when they were still little. They do not know me. Philip is raising them to be working-class rats." He turned to her. "Lady Arabella, would you agree that this is an intolerable situation?"

Arabella gripped her hands. "I won't allow you to call them animals. They are lovely, well-behaved children, living a happy life, Your Grace."

"Bah. Happy! Philip has a duty. When I kick the bucket, which is going to be very soon, mark you, he's going to be the twenty-sixth Duke of Morley. Whether he wants to or not. He can run away to the farthest ends of the earth, and he will still be the twenty-sixth Duke of Morley. Little Robin, ah, what a bright, charming boy! Little Robin will be the twenty-seventh Duke of Morley. But Lady Arabella. Look at them. Look at them! No manners, no breeding whatsoever. No pride!" He groaned. "Not an inkling of awareness of who they really are."

He turned to Arabella and there was agony on his face. "Philip refuses to see me. He denies my name, his own inheritance, his entire legacy. His fortune! He could eat each meal with a different set of golden cutleries if he wanted. I have an entire closet full of them. Instead, he prefers to eat poor man's bread with his hands."

The old man broke off and suddenly crumbled into a heap of misery.

"He won't let me greet his children. My great-grandchildren! When I meet them on the street, he pretends we are strangers. What have I done to deserve such contrary, unnatural offspring," he moaned and burst into tears.

Arabella found herself kneeling by his chair on the floor. "There, there," she crooned. From a horrid old man, he'd suddenly turned into a lonely and sad child. His sobs racked his bony body. This physical exertion couldn't be good for him.

She looked up helplessly at Mrs Stanyon, who handed her

a napkin, which she gave to the duke. With shaking hands, he pressed it against his eyes.

"Ah, Lady Arabella. My life hasn't been easy." Tears kept pooling out of his grey-green eyes and rolled over his papery skin. "I have made so many mistakes. Too many to count."

"We all make mistakes, sir." She patted his hand.

"Mine are so grave I lost my entire family." The sigh torn from his heart seemed genuine. It touched her. "He won't give me a chance to atone." He suddenly grabbed her hand tightly. "All I want is his forgiveness. I want to hear it from his lips before I die." He squeezed her hands so tightly, she almost cried out. "Will you help me, Lady Arabella?"

"But how?" Arabella wasn't sure she ought to meddle in this. This was between Philip and his grandfather.

"Help me meet them. Help me set up a chance to talk to them. That's all I ask of you. A chance."

A chance. Everyone deserved a chance.

She'd fought for a chance at taking reins into her own hand so she could shape her own life. But meddling in someone else's life? That was something different. Arabella hesitated as she thought of Philip. How stubborn he was. How intelligent. The way his eyes lit up when he talked of his inventions, or when he played with his children. Once or twice, she'd seen the same light in his eyes when he talked with her.

A slight smile played about the old man's lips. "You love him."

The words reverberated in the quiet room as if he'd blared them out with a trumpet.

Arabella jumped up. "I do not!"

"Balderdash. I wonder what your esteemed brother will say to this?" His eyes gleamed with cunning.

"You're blackmailing me."

"Am I? With my eighty years I know love when I see it. It's in the eyes. Yours have that feverish glow a woman in love has. I have seen it countless times." He waved his hand as if to dismiss it. "Mind you, not that love was something that I lived by myself. Far from it." He leaned forward. "That may have been my biggest mistake. Not permitting myself to ever feel an inkling of love for my own flesh and blood. How deeply I regret that now. I have lost them for it, Lady Arabella. I no longer ask. I beg you to help me not to lose my grandson."

Arabella wrung her hands. Feelings she could barely understand coursed through her.

This man, with Philip's eyes, was difficult to refuse. Everyone deserved a chance.

"What do you want me to do?" she heard herself say.

CHAPTER 18

The steering axis and the point of contact between the front wheel and the ground must be perpendicular. Check. Philip sketched a quick calculation on a sheet of paper with his pencil.

The value must be equal to the numerator — when she laughed, like yesterday in the lake, a tiny dimple formed at the corner of her mouth. It was adorable.

Adorable? Confound it. He had maggots in his head. *Focus, Philip, focus.* Where was he?

Numerator. Yes. The value has to be equal to — or was it denominator? Better double check. That number was off. It should be — where was she, anyway? She'd been gone for most of the afternoon. She said she'd take a walk. 'Pon his soul, it wasn't any of his bloody business what she did during her free time. She could walk all the way to London if she wanted. Provided she was back in the evening, safe and sound.

He sketched a few numbers down, annoyed at the short stub of the pencil. He swore. Imagine a pencil that one didn't have to sharpen. A mechanical writing device, yes. Something with a mechanism that propelled the lead forward as it was being used …would save him heaps of time constantly having to sharpen his pencil. He grabbed another sheet and sketched down his idea. Now he had two calculations to work on simultaneously.

A walk didn't take three hours. He'd seen her head off in the direction of the main road.

Maybe she'd gone to the cliffs. What if she didn't know the cliffs were there? What if she fell?

Bah. She was naive and the worst liar he'd encountered in his entire life, but she wasn't stupid. Of course, she wouldn't fall down that cliff.

But what if a thunderstorm came again? He swallowed. He went out and searched the flawless blue sky until he saw a tiny white cloud in the distance. That's it. He'd have to go out and look for her.

"Peggy, I'll be back shortly, the children are out in the back," he called as he opened the door.

"Yes, sir," she shouted from the kitchen, where she was baking pie.

In the end he didn't have to go far. He saw her slim figure walking down the road, and they met before he even reached the curve.

"Miss Weston!" Dash it, he didn't have any business feeling so relieved at seeing her.

"Mr Merivale." Did he imagine it, or did an odd look cross her face when she saw him? "I just walked a bit over there —" She made a vague motion with her hand. "It is so pretty there, over the meadow, and I lost all track of time. Is anything amiss?"

"Yes. No. Everything is fine. I was just thinking, a thunderstorm. You know."

Her eyes went to the blue sky. "It doesn't look like it will storm any time soon."

124

"Not now, but there is a cloud forming over there." He pointed to the tiny cloud above. "Wouldn't want you caught in a storm again." He cleared his throat. "All that thunder."

"But that looks harmless."

"Deceptive, Miss Weston. Deceptive. The tiny harmless thing could develop into a thunderstorm of tremendous proportion within minutes." He was garbling nonsense. *Pull yourself together, Philip.*

"Ah. If you say so." She pulled off her straw bonnet and fanned herself. His heart started to hammer in a way it shouldn't. Dash it if he didn't stare at her, smitten — like a lovelorn schoolboy.

"Confound it." He had no business thinking thoughts like this!

Startled, she drew away. "Excuse me?"

"I beg your pardon. Zounds. I have maggots in my brain." He shook his head as if that would help clear him of those unsettling thoughts. "I haven't been able to concentrate all day. It's one of those days."

"What are you working on?" She seemed genuinely interested.

His spirits lifted. "It's an invention of a kind that will certainly revolutionise the world, Miss Weston. Come, I will show you the prototype."

Philip led her to the shed and pulled a cloth off a big, bulky device. "What do you think it is?"

She tilted her head sideways and frowned. "It has two wheels so it must be a vehicle. They are held together by this wooden lattice, and it has something that looks like a seat. And this handlebar is where you put your hands? Is someone meant to sit on it and steer it?"

"You are brilliant, Miss Weston. Watch." He pulled the vehicle between his legs, held the handles and pushed it along the ground with his feet. "It would be even better if it could have a mechanical means of propelling itself forward — I am working on that — but as a start, this is quite something, wouldn't you say?"

"It's amazing." Miss Weston gaped at him. "I have never seen anything like it! It will make horses superfluous one day."

"You understand the gist of it! As a means of transportation without horsepower, yes. Do you want to try it?"

She looked like she very much wanted to, but then pointed to her skirts. "If you could devise one that women can use? The skirts will be in the way and entangle themselves with the wheels."

He scratched his head. "Fair point. It ought to be possible to design something with a lower bar ... but then the axis ..."

Again, there was this odd look on her face. "Mr Merivale?"

"Hmm?"

"Can I ask you something?"

Philip beamed at her. "Anything, my dear. Anything." As far as he was concerned, she could ask the sun of him and he'd get it down for her. After he'd invented a device to get it down.

She took a deep breath. "Why didn't you tell me that you are the Earl of Threthewick?"

He felt like she'd thrown a bucket with ice water over him. "What?"

She pressed a hand to her throat. "You are the Earl of Threthewick."

"How do you know that?"

She evaded his eyes. "The other day someone delivered a missive for the Earl of Threthewick. I assumed it had been sent to the wrong address. I set the letter aside. Then I saw you read it."

"I am not the Earl of Threthewick." His voice sounded flat

and didn't reflect the turmoil he felt inside. An ugly, snaky feeling unfurled at the pit of his stomach. Was she spying on him?

"My lord?"

Philip's head whipped around. "Don't you *ever* call me that! No one *ever* calls me that, do you hear?"

Arabella took a step back. No wonder. He'd snarled at her. He'd probably bared his teeth at her too, like a beast, and was this a growling sound that came out of his mouth?

"I'm sorry. I need to look for the children," she babbled, backing away further.

Then she turned and fled.

He slammed a hand on the wooden working table.

Blast.

CHAPTER 19

*A*rabella regretted the question as soon as it was out of her mouth. One moment he'd smiled at her sunnily, the other his face shut down like someone had drawn a black oilcloth over it. That look of mistrust on his face still disconcerted her. He'd regarded her as if she were a stranger. Worse. An enemy.

He'd *growled* at her. She rubbed her eyebrows. No one ever growled at her!

She'd wanted to mention in a straightforward manner that she'd had tea with the duke, for whatever was wrong with that? And that the duke very much wanted to meet Philip and his family. If Philip declined, there was nothing she could do about it. But then he'd reacted in such a violent way when she brought up his title, that she deemed it wiser to not mention Morley. In fact, she was now certain Philip would dismiss her unconditionally if he found out she'd had tea with him.

She wondered how she was going to be able to arrange a meeting between him and his grandfather. She didn't like Morley very much, but she felt a small pang of sympathy for the old man if he always encountered such hostility from Philip.

Arabella chewed on her bottom lip as doubt assailed her. Maybe she should forget about acting as a go-between. It really was none of her business. But the duke had asked her, no, begged her for help. She found it difficult to decline. She'd have to arrange a meeting somehow without Philip learning she'd ever met Morley.

She was doing this for the children, she told herself. They had grown very dear to her, the children. And Philip…

"You are in love with him," the duke had said.

"No, I am not," she said out loud. But her heart flipped, her hands grew sweaty, and her entire body hummed like she'd swallowed a beehive.

"I am just hungry," she concluded. That was it, yes. Tea would fix this.

She decided to go to the kitchen. "I would love to have a cup of tea, Peggy." Arabella cut herself off and gaped.

A bear of a man stood in front of the stove. "Me too, lass, me too." He spoke with a distinct Scottish burr in the deepest voice she'd heard in her entire life. "Peggy's not here so one has to lend a hand oneself. Water's almost boiling."

His face looked weather-beaten and rugged, marking him as an outdoor man, but he wore well-fashioned, clean clothes.

"Who are you?" she asked, taken aback.

The man appraised her with sharp eyes under bushy eyebrows. Dodging the question, he replied, "So Philip's finally got himself a lass?"

She felt a fiery blush cover her cheeks. "Oh no. I am the governess. Miss Arabella Weston." She waited for the man to introduce himself.

"Guverness. Huh." The man turned to take the kettle off the

stove. He poured water in the chipped tea pot. He seemed entirely at home in the kitchen with a quiet authority that made her wonder whether he was a friend or colleague of Philip.

"Are you–?"

"Teacups are over there," he interrupted, jutting his chin into the cupboard to the right.

Oh. He expected her to set the table for tea.

She got them out and set them on the kitchen table.

"What're ye doing?" The man drew his bushy eyebrows together.

She paused in setting down the teacup. "Setting the table for tea?"

"In the parlour, lass, in the parlour," he growled. "Like proper people that we are. Assuming the room is inhabitable."

"Right." She'd almost forgotten the original purpose of the parlour.

She carried the teacups to the parlour and cleared the table off the books, quills and papers from this morning's lesson.

The big man followed with a tray of piping hot tea and a plate of biscuits, which he must have dug out from some closet.

Arabella straightened her gown and turned to him. "May I inquire as to who you are, sir?"

She heard footsteps. Philip stood by the door.

"This, Miss Weston, is Fergus McAllister." Philip's face broke into a big smile. "My grandfather."

The man opened both his arms wide. Philip walked into the older man's embrace.

Arabella plopped into a chair.

Grandfather? Another one? How many grandfathers could a man Philip's age have? This man didn't look old enough to be a grandfather. He was big, his deeply tanned face was wizened, and he had a youthful energy about him.

He thumped Philip on the back. "Pip, my boy. How you've grown." Philip snorted into his shoulder.

"You haven't seen your grandfather in a while?" Arabella enquired. One had to say something, after all, in this unorthodox situation.

The man counted on his fingers. "It's been a while. Too long. A good four months."

"Five. You helped us move the things from London, if you recall."

"Aye." Fergus nodded. "Many things happened in the meantime. I see ye got yerself a guverness." He nodded at Arabella, who was pouring tea. "Smart move."

"Yes. Katy did, actually."

His bright, sharp eyes were on her. "If she's a guverness, then I'm a dairy maid."

Arabella, who took had just taken a sip of her tea, started to cough.

Philip responded with something which she didn't understand, and Fergus replied in kind, which she understood even less. The words flew back and forth, and she could only watch with open mouth.

"Granda speaks Scots, Gaelic and English," Philip explained.

"Aye, and everything mixed up together," Fergus grinned.

The door crashed open, and the children rushed in.

"Graaaaaanda!" They hurled themselves at him. Joy crawled into his lap, Robin climbed onto his back and chattered to him about his flying machine, Katy hung onto his arm and inquired whether he'd brought them presents. They chattered in a mix of Scots and English.

"Presents, aye, and sweeties I brought and the books ye wanted, Philip. Have a look at the packages over there in the corner, children. But now let an old man drink his tea." The children let go of him, scampered off to the corner and proceeded to unwrap their gifts. Fergus pulled a flask out and added a good dollop to his teacup. "Whisky," he told Arabella with a twinkling eye. "The only proper way to drink tea." He turned to Philip, "Pip. I have a bunch of letters for ye to look through. Some of it urgent." He dug in his waist pocket and pulled out a pack, handing it to Philip.

"The patent office?" Philip snatched the letters and perused them.

Arabella fidgeted in her chair, remembering what Morley had said about Philip's patents. He'd apparently intercepted them. Didn't Philip deserve to know that? How could she tell him without giving away she'd had tea with Morley?

Deciding to leave the family to themselves, Arabella got up.

"Sit down, Miss," Fergus said, leaning back. "Guverness or no, it's none of my business. But I see yer a lady."

Apparently, the whole world knew she was a lady. She could wear a potato sack and sprinkle ash over her head and they'd still insist she was a lady. Why did she even bother pretending otherwise?

"Not that it matters. But I'm a blacksmith." Fergus winked at her.

"Ah, yes."

"I'm good at what I do."

"I'm sure you are, sir."

"He"—Fergus nodded at his grandson, who'd gone to the window to read the letters —"has learned the trade since he was a wee bairn, and now he's almost better than me. Business has never been so good. We McAllisters are generations of blacksmiths. We're proud of who we are. Philip's a true McAllister in that sense. He knows the trade as well as the best of us. He's also done something that none of us did and that is go to University. What's it ye studied again, boy?"

"Mathematics," Philip mumbled as he read the letter, his eyebrows drawn together.

"Aye. Mathematics." He sounded right proud of his grandson. "My boy's got lots of juice in here." He tapped his forehead. "He invents things that are nothing short of miraculous."

"I have seen some of his inventions. They are wonderful."

"Aye. My grandson is a blacksmith, a mathematician, an inventor." He nodded. "He's also a lord."

Arabella held her breath. Her eyes flew to Philip.

"I am not." Philip lowered his letters and glowered at his grandfather.

"Balderdash. Of course ye are. Ye dinnae like to talk about it and it's no good. Ye can't keep denying it. There's a letter in there that ye have to act on."

Philip threw the pack on the table. "There's nothing there that interests me." He tucked his hands in his armpits, which made him look like a recalcitrant schoolboy.

With a glance, Arabella saw that they were all addressed to the Earl of Threthewick.

"The letter from the patent office isn't in there." Philip scowled.

"No." His grandfather shuffled through the letters and pulled one out.

"This one. Read this one."

"It doesn't interest me."

"Stubborn boy. Well, I've read it, knowing that he never would." He lifted a missive and waved it in his hand. "It's from the Earl of Winchester."

Arabella's head perked up. She knew that name. An acquaintance of her brother's.

Philip shrugged. "Don't know no earl."

"No ye don't, but ye ought. He's keen on meeting ye."

"Bah. If he wants to meet me, he should come here."

"Listen boy. This Earl of Winchester is not the usual man. He's connections to the patent's office. He's interested in inventions and the patron of many inventors. He's the driving force behind a society for engineers."

Philip's head whipped up.

"Doesn't live far from here. He's giving a dinner party. Wants Threthewick to attend." He threw the letter back on the table. "And I say, he is goin'."

Philip swallowed as he stared at the letter.

"Tuck away your stubbornness and read the letter, boy. It could be the very thing that ye need."

"I've always said I would do this on my own and never use *that* name to drive my interests forward."

"Haud yer weesht. Dinnae be a gowk."

Philip replied something in kind, and they were soon in a heated debate.

"Let me tell ye one thing, Philip. I can take yer precious device to London tomorrow and deposit it at the patent office, together with the money. And ye'll never see it again. Like what happened to all yer inventions."

Philip set his lips in a mulish line. "We know it takes a while for them to process things. It could take years."

"I think your grandfather is right." Arabella hadn't intended to speak up.

Philip stared at her. "What do you know about those things?"

"Not much," she said, "but your grandfather's correct when he says that the right connection usually opens doors. Especially in London. I've heard, or rather read, about Winchester. He has a reputation for being eccentric and forward-thinking. He's uncommonly open-minded towards scientists and inventors. It might be a good idea to go, if he's invited you — or rather, Threthewick."

"Aye." The old man nodded. "Pull yerself together, go to that dinner, talk to the earl and tell him about yer invention and ask him to use his influence. Not that the future Duke of Morley would ever have to beg anyone's patronage in anything," he snorted.

"Don't ever utter that name in my house." Philip snarled.

"Aye, that's another thing. Get over him already. Ye've been living in a fantasy world here and as long as that works for ye, fine. But what about the children?"

The children were quiet but while Robin and Joy played, Katy was sitting on the floor, following their conversation. It was clear from the lack of surprise on her face that she must've known about this.

Suddenly the puzzle pieces came together, and Arabella understood. Katy knew that Morley was her grandfather. She knew she was going to be a duke's daughter one day. She'd been shamed at her last visit at Thornton Hall. That was why Katy wanted a governess so desperately.

A flush of angry colour suffused Philip's face. "Never." He threw the letter on the table and stormed out of the room.

Fergus folded his arms and nodded, satisfied. "Dinnae fash yersel. He'll come round. We might need yer help, Miss."

"My help?" That was the second grandfather within a day who was soliciting her help.

He nodded. "The boy needs to be turned into a lord. Ye need to help him."

"Aside from the fact that he doesn't want that, why do you think I am even remotely qualified to do this?"

"Because yer a lady."

CHAPTER 20

*P*hilip missed dinner.

It had been a simple affair which Mr Fergus prepared, consisting of a loaf of bread, cheese and butter. The children went to bed soon after, and Arabella heard Philip's low voice as he read to them. He must've returned without her noticing it.

"Join us in the parlour, Miss Weston." Fergus held the door open to her.

She hesitated. "Surely you would like to spend some time alone with your grandson?"

Fergus made an impatient movement with his hands. "We've matters to discuss."

Arabella went in, curious.

Philip joined soon after. He ran one hand through his hair, mussing it up even further.

"The book's long finished, but Joy can't bear the story to be over, so I just have to keep inventing a continuation," he said with a lopsided grin. "I pretend I'm reading it."

Fergus nodded. "Yer a good father, Pip."

"If I'm a good father it's because I had a good role model." The two men grinned at each other.

"Before we talk. Port? Whisky?" Philip lifted the dusty bottle that he'd set on the table when he came into the room.

"Yer port is hideous, and yer whisky is watery," Fergus announced. "Give me a glass of my own stuff that I brought down. This is my *aqua vitae.* Water for life."

Philip poured him a glass of the whisky from the bottle he'd brought. He poured a second glass and handed it to Arabella who looked at it with wide eyes. Ladies didn't drink whisky. It was improper. They were supposed to drink lemonade and tea and ratafia. Maybe a sip of red wine but whisky? The thought was outrageous. She stared at the copper liquid in the glass. What would it taste like?

"Take it," the old man's rusty voice commanded. "It's good for yer constitution."

Philip cocked an eyebrow at her as he held the glass out.

Her hand reached out on its own and took the glass. She swirled the caramel-coloured liquid.

"Take small sips," Philip advised.

It tasted hideous. She pulled a face. It left a warm trail down her throat and pooled in the stomach. She took a second sip. Surprisingly, that tasted better.

"Sit down, Pip. Right. Now tell Miss Weston exactly what's been going on." Turning to Arabella, Fergus said, "One of my main rules in the family is: never have a secret. Always talk things out before ye go to bed. This is such a time."

Philip dropped with a sigh into a chair. "A few months ago —"

"Earlier," Fergus crossed his arms.

Philip grumbled. "Two years ago —"

"All the way back." Fergus shook his head. "Git oan wae it." Philip scowled.

"I see yer not going to do this properly. Let me begin.

We're starting with Philip's father. The Duke of Morley's son."

Arabella averted her eyes. It wasn't a good moment to tell them she already knew the story as she'd talked to the other grandfather. She was curious about their version, however.

"So, Philip's father, Edward, was to become the next Duke of Morley after his brother died. Married my Marian, who came down from the north to visit my sister Joan, who lived here." Fergus shook his head. "Strange how life goes sometimes. My sister's husband died at sea, so Marian went to stay with her for a while. My sister Joan passed on long since. So did Marian. She was a bonnie lass." He stared morosely at the fireplace. "Barely eighteen."

Arabella nodded. Philip's mother had been a blacksmith's daughter who'd come to the village to stay with her grieving aunt. She could see how things must've developed from there. The duke had said she was a laundry maid, a "rat in the gutter." It would've been easy to meet the duke's son, who was restless and had a penchant for roaming the countryside.

Philip jumped up and leaned against the mantle of the fireplace, his face averted in the shadow so she couldn't see it. The soft light of the candle that stood next to him on the mantelpiece flickered a copper sheen over thick locks of auburn hair that curled in his neck.

"Then she met Edward," Arabella said softly. She could very well imagine how a girl like Marian McAllister would've been swept off her feet by a dashing earl who courted her. Especially if he resembled Philip.

Fergus sighed. "Love at first sight and all that. Can't say I was happy about the union. Ran away to Gretna Green. Settled down right here in this hut."

"This was your parents' cottage?"

Philip nodded. "My father owned it. That's why I love this

place so much." He patted the grey stone wall with a hand. "I was born here."

"Aye, then came a wee bairn, this strapping lad here, before any of us could blink. The duke, however, was furious."

"I can imagine," Arabella murmured.

"Tried to prove the marriage wasn't valid. But it was. Edward was wild but intelligent. Made sure the paperwork was in order. There was nothing the duke could've done. Didn't disinherit Edward but made life miserable for them. Showed up every day in the carriage, treated my Marian like she was dirt beneath his boots. So, one night, the young family packed up and left for London. In secret. He wasn't to know of their whereabouts. Aye, for a while that went well. But the duke, he has his people, and he has power. And from here on, Pip, it's yer turn to tell the story." Fergus leaned back.

Arabella saw Philip chew on the insides of his cheeks. Then he downed the remains of his whisky and spoke in a low voice.

"Father did well in the city. He was working in various accounting firms in London. Mother made lace at home. She was very good at that. I had a happy childhood, Miss Weston. My parents were wonderful people. They loved each other dearly, and they provided a home for me full of love, laughter, and security. The only thing I ever wanted was an older brother who'd take me fishing." A corner of his mouth quirked up. "My parents tried to fulfil my every wish, but that was a bit beyond their ability."

"The name Merivale, where does that come from?"

"It is my father's legal name. Edward Merivale. I thought of taking on McAllister, but I wanted to honour my father by keeping the name. I've always associated Merivale more with my father than with *him*."

"What happened then?"

"Father died." Philip swallowed. "A carriage accident. He'd gotten under the wheel of a barouche. I was seven."

"I'm so sorry," Arabella whispered.

"It happened some days before school started. Father had wanted to send me to a grammar school in London. I could already read and write and already showed a marked tendency for mathematics. After the accident, Mother insisted I continue to go to school. I had to walk there on my own, it wasn't too far away. On the third day, a carriage stopped next to me. Before I could say a word, a man jumped out and dragged me in."

Arabella gasped. "He kidnapped you?"

A bitter line formed on Philip's mouth. "Yes. My father's father — I refuse to call him grandfather — kidnapped me. I was next in line, wasn't I?"

"He's a right old bawbag." Fergus nodded.

"There was a sinister-looking old man in black skulking in one corner of the carriage and a giant who tied me up, because I struggled, kicked, fought, and bit like a wild animal. In the end he drugged me with opium to make me compliant." His face darkened.

Arabella clasped her hands over her mouth. Naturally, the duke hadn't told her that particular version.

"I must've been knocked out for several days. My guess is that whenever I showed signs of waking, they fed me the stuff to knock me out again. When I finally awoke, I found myself in a tremendous bed in a dark room. The old man sitting by the bed claimed he was my grandfather. He wanted to raise me to become a proper duke, he said. I needed to learn manners. Get a proper education. He saw I was terrified of the dark and loud noises and said I needed to toughen up. My mother had raised me into a milk sop — he called her a 'rat in the gutter.' They tore me out of bed in the middle of the night, left me alone in the park, shivering, in my night-gown. I thought, what kind of a strange game is that? Then a sudden shout from the right: 'Watch out, a wolf is coming!' and shots." Philip shuddered. "There wasn't any wolf, of course. And the shots, I didn't know where they were coming from. I was just a little boy. Maybe they were just pistol shots, but to me, they sounded like cannonballs hurtling over my head. The randomness of it, in the darkness, not knowing where the next shot was coming from, it was terrifying. I curled up on the ground and cried. Morley wasn't impressed."

Arabella burned with indignation. "How terrible! What on earth was he thinking?"

"That was his way of toughening me up. A duke is never afraid of anything. Only God and the king are above him. Behave in that manner." His face darkened. "Well. I was afraid of lots of things. The dark. Sudden shots, thunder. I was most afraid of never seeing my mother again. I tried to escape. Again and again. It never worked. He had bars attached to my window. I had someone watching me day and night. I refused to eat." He shrugged. "He could be stubborn but so could I. They tried to force food into me. I spat it out again. His wife, the duchess, was a faded old lady who seemed to sympathise, but other than making me sit straight at tea and patting my hand now and then, she did not move a finger to help me. She was terrified of him, too."

His wife. The one he said who'd died so conveniently.

"With a perverted kind of logic, one may understand where the man is coming from. He sees in me the continuation of a legacy, his heritage. Of course, he wanted me raised in his image. Especially after his own sons failed him so. But what I can't forgive is the way he treated my mother. She came to plead for me. She begged him to let me go, to see whether they could reach a compromise. He refused. Then he went and killed her."

Arabella gasped. "How?"

"He threatened to have the hounds set on her if she didn't leave. I know this because a footman, who witnessed it, told me afterwards. She fled, stumbled, and fell down the stairs. She broke her neck. I lost my father, my mother, and my unborn sibling within a span of half a year. She was eight months with child."

"I am so, so sorry." A tear glided down Arabella's cheek.

Fergus patted her hand. "As terrible as it sounds, this story has a happy end."

Philip looked at him with affection. "Aye. Eventually this old man here came and rescued me. Thank God."

"How did you do it?"

Fergus cracked his knuckles, one by one. "After that miserable scumbag killed my Marian, I planned a cloak and dagger operation. I'm a blacksmith, after all. Do ye think a lock and some iron bars keep me from gettin' into a room?" He laughed a rusty laugh. "One or two servants who could no longer stand to see how they treated my Pip also helped. We got him out before the old man turned in his creaky bed. I left a dagger next to him on his pillow. As a reminder that I could've used it on him but didn't. I took Pip to the far north. The duke's powers didn't reach that far. We were hiding for the first few years. After several years, I decided it was nonsense to always be on the run, always be hiding. Face your enemy, I say. So, I went down to him and came in the same way I rescued Pip: through the window. Stood over his bed as he slept. I could've killed him. As revenge for my daughter. But I didn't. He tried to intimidate me, but I saw the fear in his eyes. Made him swear on his life that he would leave us alone." He smiled at Philip. "It worked. Pip grew up to be the prime fellow you see here." He patted his arm. "Got an excellent education. When it became clear school was too easy for him, I engaged only the best tutors for him. Learned to speak English as cleanly as any of the 'nobs in London. I made sure of that. But Pip kenned more than his tutor in mathematics. Got himself a scholarship at the University of Edinburgh. Which he breezed through in record time. And like his father, got himself married when he was still a whelp."

"Hm. How old were you when you married, Granda?" Philip asked with a grin.

"Seventeen. Don't change the topic."

"Jenny and I were married when we were both twenty-two."

His grandfather sniffed. "Pups."

"Then Katy came and Robin, and then I enlisted. To save the country from the French beast."

"You ran away, my boy, you ran away."

A pink colour crawled up Philip's neck. "I did not. That has nothing to do with the topic at hand."

"I dinna blame ye. But back to the topic." He turned to Arabella. "The buffoon of a duke never realised that this boy here is extraordinarily intelligent. Unthinkable what he would've done to him if I hadn't gotten him out. He'd have squashed his spirit. My boy here is a brilliant inventor." Fergus frowned. "The odd thing is that none of his inventions are gettin' through the patent office. They send a check but never the patent. Odd."

Arabella cleared her throat. "Maybe the duke has had a hand in it. If he is as evil as you say, I wouldn't be surprised if he meddled. Somehow." She looked down at her fingernails.

Both men stared at her.

"By Jove. He could be involved in some way," Philip said slowly.

Fergus leaned forward with a crafty look on his face. "Exactly. Which is why ye need to play in the same way."

"Granda. We've been through this. I've sworn not to make a career using his money or his name." He set his mouth in an obstinate line.

"That name would open doors for ye." Fergus knocked on the table.

"I will make my way using the name Merivale and not Morley."

"You wouldn't. Ye'd use yer father's name. The Earl of Threthewick was your father, too." Fergus' eyes bored into Philip's. "Which ye are now." Philip opened his mouth to deny it. Then he suddenly snapped it shut.

"Think of yer father, boy," Fergus insisted. "Not *him*. Forget him. Yer father never renounced his name, did he?"

"No. He never used it, either." His expression was a mask of stone.

"There is no shame in usin' yer father's name if it helps achieve yer goal."

Philip pulled on his hair. "Even if I were to agree, there is no way this would ever work. How do you see this working?"

Fergus leaned back in his chair, with a small smile. "Easy. She'll teach ye."

Both men looked at Arabella, who'd followed the interaction between the two men with amused confusion.

"What exactly am I to teach him?" She looked from one to the other.

"Teach him how to be a bleedin' earl."

Philip threw up his hands and groaned.

"Then ye go to that earl's dinner party. Ask to be admitted to the Society of Engineers. Ask him to intervene at the patent's office. One thing leads to another. It's easy as pie." Fergus nodded.

"Dinner party with the 'nobs." Philip shuddered.

Fergus patted his shoulder. "It's time ye learn to be an earl. See it as it is. A role ye play."

"When do we start?" Arabella threw him a tentative look.

"Tomorrow." Fergus got up and picked up the candle. "Until then, guid nicht."

CHAPTER 21

"What do I need so many spoons for?" Philip sat in the chair and stared at the table with misgiving. Learning table manners from Miss Weston made him feel like a boor.

Miss Weston had collected all the chipped porcelain plates, bowls, cups, and silverware she could find in the cottage and arranged them in a certain order. A teacup, a whisky glass, and a wine glass represented the different glasses that were at a formal dinner table. The silverware was limited, so there were more spoons than other utensils.

"I couldn't find enough forks, so you just have to imagine that some of these spoons are, in fact, forks. This one is for salad, fish, and meat. This one here," she touched the little fork on top of the plate, "is for cake. And this one here," she pointed to another spoon on the other side of the plate, "is your oyster fork. Imagine that it is a smaller fork with only three prongs." She pointed at the glasses. "You will have a champagne flute, a glass for white wine, one for red wine, and one for cordial sherry. A coffee or teacup and a demi-tasse will be brought in by the footmen afterwards."

Philip shook his head, bewildered.

"I filled some of them with water to make it more real. The footmen will bring and refill your glasses." After a thought, she added, "I recommend that you take a minute to observe what your neighbour does and just copy him or her. Speaking of which, you only converse with your neighbour on the right until tables are turned, then you turn to your neighbour on the left. Never talk to the person across from the table. And never converse with the footmen!"

He curled his lips in derision. "What tosh."

"It's how things are done in those circles."

He crossed his arms behind his head to test her reaction. It came promptly.

"You'd never do that at the dinner table," Arabella scolded.

He dropped his hands. Devil take it. He'd never remember all those rules. "One should just invent one device to use instead of…" he counted.

"Thirteen."

Arabella shrugged. "It's table etiquette. Dinner at court is even more formal."

Dinner at court? He sat up. "Miss Weston, are you saying you've been to dinner with the Regent?"

"Of course not." She averted her eyes. Then she looked up into his face and met his gaze frankly. "It's common knowledge. There are pictures of court table settings in every etiquette book. Regardless of whether you'll ever be attending a court function, one needs to know those things."

Philip wrinkled his forehead. She'd said her father was a baron. Were barons ever invited to court? Or their daughters? He supposed she was right that one needed to know these things. He felt like an oaf.

He tipped a finger against a knife that lay across a smaller plate on the left. "What's this for?"

"That's the butter knife. In reality it'll be smaller, wider and not as sharp."

Philip sighed. His blacksmith instruments were less complicated than this.

"You're an intelligent man. You'll figure it out. What you need to know is that your table partner will be assigned to you by the hostess, and you will enter the dining room with her together."

"I'll have to offer her my arm, I suppose, when we enter the dining room," he grumbled.

"Yes, but there's a certain order to this as well. The ones with the higher title go first. You're quite high up, so be prepared." Arabella quirked a smile and for a second her dimple appeared, which he thought charming. He decided to make her smile more.

"Order?"

"Dukes, marquesses, earls, followed by the rest of the guests in order of precedence."

He rolled his eyes.

"Yes, I know you don't care a tuppence for this, but it's the way it is. Back to what is in front of you. Repeat what each of these are for." She pointed at the glasses.

He cleared his throat and attempted to identify the purpose of each glass.

"It will do" She furrowed her brow. "Now, after dinner, the gentlemen remain to smoke and drink port, whereas the ladies retire to a separate room."

"Why?"

She blinked. "Because. It's always been done this way. I suppose it isn't seemly for men to be smoking in the presence of women."

"I don't smoke, so I can go and have coffee with the women?"

"No!"

"Why?"

"Because the men only join them after they've had their smoke and their port. Elbows off the table!"

He removed his elbows. "It seems mightily strange to me. And then?"

"Then, after the men are done with —" she waved a pale hand. "whatever it is they do, they join the women, and they have coffee together."

"Why?"

"You're worse than Robin." A smile lurked on her lips. "You are doing this on purpose."

"What?" He looked at her with mock, wide-eyed innocence.

"Pretending to be more stupid than you really are."

A chuckle escaped him. "It's because I enjoy seeing you flustered, Miss Weston."

To his delight, she blushed prettily. His spirits soared.

"You take this rather seriously, don't you?"

"It is very important, Mr Merivale. I want you to succeed."

He shook his head. "I wonder whether it wouldn't be easier if I just call on the fellow."

"Yes, you can call on his lordship the day *after* the dinner. To follow up on any kind of agreement you may have made with him during the after dinner port session. This is where you bring up the topic of your invention."

"Not during supper?"

She shook her head. "The earl will sit at the head of the table, and while you will sit in his vicinity, it is your job to keep your table lady entertained. Focus your conversation on her, then on the neighbour on the other side."

He groaned. "I have no idea how to do this."

Arabella shrugged. "Just be yourself."

"You know that when I am myself, I keep rambling on

about my inventions. I may be a social boor, but even I know that the lady won't be amused."

"Right. You need a battle plan." She bit her lip. He noticed that her two front teeth were infinitesimally crooked. Another detail that made her charming.

"A battle plan sounds good." He leaned on his elbow again. She pushed it away.

"First, you talk about the weather. Then, you enquire as to whether she enjoys the food. You can comment on each dish, in fact, but don't overdo it. Then — oh, I don't know." Arabella thought for a moment. "Women usually like it when men flatter them."

"Flatter. Hm. Let's assume you are my table companion, and I am going to attempt conversation." He cleared his throat, bent forward and stared intensely into her eyes. "Did you know that your eyes are not exactly blue? There are fire-golden sprinkles around the iris, like stardust swirling in the infinite summer night's sky, wild and free." He observed, fascinated, how her eyes widened.

"What are you doing?" she whispered.

"I am making table talk. I am flattering you." He tilted his head to one side. "Did it work?"

A deep flush spread over her pale face. "It's the most beautiful thing anyone has ever told me."

"Good." He leaned back, satisfied.

She shook herself. "But it is entirely inappropriate for a dinner conversation. This was a flirtation. Quite another thing altogether." Her voice took on the censorious tone of the governess.

"But you said I should flatter women!" He grinned.

"You had better stick to the weather. Or even better, just get her to talk, and you listen. Women like good listeners."

"Capital plan, indeed." Philip observed with interest that

she was still flustered. He placed one elbow on the table and propped his chin on his hand.

She pulled his arm away. "Never, ever put your elbows on the table. Sit up straight. Chin up. Arms to your body."

"She's worse than a field marshal," he muttered to himself. "I can't see the food on my plate if I have to keep my chin up. I'll be looking directly at the flower arrangement or the person on the other side to whom I am not supposed to talk."

Arabella sighed.

"In all seriousness. How am I to eat my soup in this manner? Navigating it to my mouth will be a science. I'll dribble it all over my expensive waistcoat."

Speaking of which. Granda had brought an entire wardrobe with him. He must've planned this far ahead of time. Philip growled.

"For heaven's sake. Don't growl, don't slurp, don't burp or make any other ungentlemanly sound. Eat your soup like this." Of course, she did it perfectly. Dipping her spoon into an imaginary soup, lifting it up to her lips, sipping from it without making as much as a sound. His eyes were glued to those pale pink lips of hers.

He shook himself.

Spoon. Soup. Right. Blast it if he couldn't do this.

"No growling, my lord," she warned.

He dropped the spoon. "Don't call me that."

"My lord. You need to get used to this address."

He glared at her. "If you call me *my lord* again, I will slurp, burp, growl, and fart my way through dinner."

A peal of laughter escaped her. Her eyes sparked bright blue with the challenge. "No you won't — *my lord*."

He dipped the spoon into the glass and flicked a spoonful of water into her face.

She spluttered.

He roared with laughter.

Miss Weston wasn't amused. She got up, picked up the glass and dumped the content right over his head.

Rivulets of cold water ran down his neck.

He spluttered.

She laughed.

He pulled out a handkerchief and wiped his face. "You fight unfairly, escalating in this excessive manner." Then he stared. "It is true, you know."

She sobered. "What is?"

"You have stardust in your eyes. And when you are happy and laugh, like now, they turn into shooting stars."

He could drown in her eyes. His gaze focused on her lips, which had opened slightly and which seemed very close. He leaned forward.

Then they heard the door outside open, followed by the trampling of footsteps and laughter. Fergus just returned with the children. Just in time.

He jerked back.

Arabella tucked an invisible strand of hair behind her ear. "Where were we? Next on the curriculum: dance." She sounded breathless.

"Oh, no, no, no." He raked both hands through his hair.

"Yes. I'd like Katy and your grandfather to join in. The more the merrier."

Philip groaned. Something told him that holding Arabella in his arms for a waltz was going to be a very bad idea.

CHAPTER 22

t turned into a merry evening. Philip's grandfather could play the fiddle, Arabella played a tune on the piano and then attempted to teach Philip and the children the basic steps of a country dance, interspersed by Fergus' words of advice.

"Never say we Scots aren't dancers." Fergus grinned.

"We know how to dance a Ceilidh so this can't be much more difficult," Katy told her. Her cheeks were red with excitement. She grasped the two– hand turn quickly.

Not so her father, who had two left feet.

"I will just remain sitting during the dancing." He groaned as he limped dramatically to a chair.

"No, my boy, you won't. The Earl of Threthewick has to stand up at least once. You don't want to be mistaken for an antisocial boor."

"I *am* an antisocial boor." Philip set his chin in a stubborn way. "And proud of it, too."

"Aye, that's the problem. I should've taught you all this earlier." Fergus sighed. "If Granma had lived longer, we'd have done it, too."

"It isn't so difficult, Mr Merivale. If you can calculate the rotational speed of a wheel, then surely you can figure out the order of the dance."

"No, I can't," he replied, testily. "Because my numbers make sense, but this doesn't. There's no rhyme and reason to this hopping." To prove his point, he stepped on Arabella's foot.

"Just avoid stepping on the lady's foot," Arabella hopped around on one foot, grimacing. "If you can manage to do that, it'd already be a feat."

"Bah."

Fergus put down his fiddle. "Next: waltz."

Philip groaned. "Have mercy, Granda."

"Ye need to learn this, son. This is something I'm good at. An Austrian taught me. A brilliant dance. The world won't be the same after ye've danced to the tunes of a proper waltz. Miss Weston, if ye please."

He pulled her into his arms, somewhat closer than what she was used to. "There's got to be more distance —" she began.

"Bah. This is where the English got it wrong. It's got to be danced closer, so ye can twirl real fast. Like this." He gathered her up to his chest and twirled her around in a breathtaking twist, humming to the tunes of a waltz. Arabella was a good dancer and light on her feet, and Fergus had a strong lead. She was used to dancing it slower, with more distance to the partner. This close, they spun faster than she ever had at any of her balls.

"This is amazing," she gasped.

"Yer as light as a feather, a joy to dance with. Now, Pip." Philip crossed his arms. But Fergus would have none of it. "Dinnae be doaty." Philip pulled himself up and imitated his steps.

"Aye, that's more like it. This is the basic box step. One,

two, three, one, two, three. Easy enough." Even Philip got that.

"Put the foot this way to turn." Philip got that, too.

"Now, together with the lady." He pushed Arabella into his arms. Philip caught her. This close, Arabella could feel the heat radiating from his body.

She stumbled.

"This time it was her, not me," Philip quipped.

"Aye, but don't stop after each step. This is a dance, so string them up together fluidly. I will sing a tune." Fergus hummed a tune. Robin and Joy were dancing alongside them, giggling, and Katy danced with Fergus. Philip turned Arabella gently and slowly. Her brain stopped functioning. There was no music, this was no ballroom, they weren't wearing ballroom attire. He stumbled and faltered, but it felt like the most heavenly dance she'd ever danced. She floated on a cotton cloud.

"Breathe," he whispered. His warm breath brushed against the little hairs above her ear.

She shivered.

Arabella exhaled in one swoop. She must've held her breath the entire time.

He swung her in one final curve and stopped. She felt his hand on her back and again forgot to breathe.

"That was magnificent!" Katy's voice intruded. "I wish I could go to a ball. I wish I could go with Papa!"

Arabella wished he'd never let her go. He dropped his hands, apparently with reluctance.

"Yer time will come, lass." Fergus said. "As for you. Just keep leading the lady."

Like Katy, Arabella suddenly wished she could go with him. How would it be, to dance with him to real music?

"Miss Weston?"

Startled, Arabella looked up.

Katy had to repeat the question twice. "I was asking whether you thought Papa did fine?"

"He's an excellent dancer after all."

"The waltz is more logical. There's mathematics behind it," he grumbled.

"Aye, and now that we've got that figured out, the next step is clothes."

"That is something I will leave to you," Arabella said hastily. She'd already seen him nearly naked once.

Twice.

She swallowed.

"Aye boy, we'll make an earl out of you yet." Fergus, giving Philip a clap on the back, was satisfied.

CHAPTER 2 3

*E*verything had gone wrong.

He'd led the wrong lady in at the wrong time, sat at the wrong place and eaten with the wrong forks. He'd mixed up the fish fork with the pudding fork. His table lady, Lady Bleckingham, who had more feathers on her headgear than she had hair, had looked at him with amusement and enquired whether "my lord" intended to skip the oysters. He'd replied he had no idea what "my lord" intended to eat next.

The lady had uttered a peal of laughter. Then he realised she'd meant him.

Blushing, he'd put the fork down, only to have a footman step in and replace it.

That liveried fellow hovered behind him, following his every move. He took a sip of his wine, the fellow refilled it. Philip wanted to help himself to a plate of meats, the fellow jumped in to hand it to him. He was probably counting the number of times he lifted his spoon or fork to his mouth, as well. It was highly irritating.

Miss Weston had said he was to comment on each dish. He racked his brains. "Perfectly symmetrically proportioned filet," he uttered in–between bites. Blast it, what interesting thing was there to say about a grey slab of meat?

He turned the fork in his hand. "Best thing I ever ate," he lied.

It worked. His table partner brightened and started describing the food she'd eaten at Lady Whitebury's supper the other night.

He breathed a sigh of relief. The problem was now and then there'd be this odd look on her face, and he knew immediately he'd blundered, but not how or why.

"My lord?"

After the third time she'd said, "my lord," it occurred to him she might mean him.

The entire table stared at him.

His fish fork, with a piece of meat on it, hovered mid-air.

His host, the earl, repeated, probably for the third time, with an amused look on his face: "I said, Threthewick may have an opinion on this."

Zounds. He'd been talking to him! He'd never get used to this blasted title.

"Opinion on what?" That came out more testily than he intended, but did they all have to look at him like he was a pimple on Jove's chin?

"On the *Savannah's* successful transoceanic voyage from America. The world's first steam-powered ship. It docked in Liverpool after only twenty-seven days."

Philip widened his eyes with interest. Now that was something he understood. "It's a naval wonder. It sailed with sails, steam engine and collapsible paddle wheels. A brilliant innovation, I wish I'd thought of it myself. They'd operated the steam-powered paddle for only eighty-five hours, but if they'd done so for a third of the time longer, the ship would've arrived least three days sooner. If not earlier. It's simple mathematics."

"They ran out of fuel," the earl remarked. "Hence it had to rely more on sail than steam."

"Imagine crossing the Atlantic on a vessel powered entirely by steam." Philip felt his cheek heat with excitement. "According to my calculations, we could travel across the ocean to America in fourteen days, maybe less."

Lord Royston shuddered. "Nothing in this world will get me to set a foot on that smoking monster. When people spotted it off the Irish coast, they thought it was on fire, on account of all the smoke. Read it in *The Times*."

"Steam." Philip stabbed his fork in the air. "Not smoke. The propulsion technology behind it is such that the fuelled boiler heats up water, and the ensuing water vapour is transmitted to the engine. I've considered a similar design for my own invention but have come to the conclusion it isn't functional for my particular purpose."

Blank, polite faces stared at him.

The earl gave him an assessing look. "Threthewick here is an engineer and inventor. You will have to tell me all about it after supper. But I am afraid we are boring the ladies with our technical talk."

Philip finally popped the fork into his mouth, satisfied. This was what he wanted.

After supper, when the men retired to the billiard room to smoke and drink port, like Miss Weston had said they would, he'd taken the earl aside and blathered his ears full with his proposed invention, to the point of grabbing a newspaper off the coffee table and sketching a basic diagram into its margins.

The earl had listened politely.

When he started to sketch, he'd followed his movements with an alert look in his eyes.

"What on earth is that?"

"That is the front wheel that can be pivoted with the lever, here."

"I mean what you are holding in your hand."

"That?" Philip twisted the metallic tube between his fingers. "Oh, that's a pencil." He shrugged. "I asked my grandfather to make it for me. He's a better blacksmith when it comes to fine work and jewellery. I am done with constantly having to sharpen the tip of my pencil, so I designed this."

"May I?" The earl held out his palm.

Philip gave it to him. "But to return to the problem at hand. I've submitted all the papers and a prototype to the patent office in London a good year ago, and it has passed the first two commissions, but now they keep delaying further examinations so it can be signed by the king. No one seems to be able to tell me what's the status quo. I don't understand it. It shouldn't take so long."

"The bureaucracy at the patent office is a nightmare. There is no rhyme and reason to it. Say, how does it work?" The earl kept fiddling around with the pencil.

Philip showed him. "I intend to submit an improved prototype shortly. I was wondering whether you could use your influence at the patent office to, er, help things along." That was awkwardly put.

"This is brilliant, Threthewick. Brilliant." The earl clicked the pencil and scribbled something on the newspaper. "The mechanism behind it?"

Philip sighed. "It's simple. The mechanism propels the lead forward." He explained it in greater detail.

"A propelling pencil that doesn't need to be sharpened. Utterly brilliant."

"Yes, yes. But my patent —"

"Did you think to get this patented?" The earl lifted the pencil.

Philip shrugged.

"You must." The earl slapped his shoulder. "You have a brilliant mind, Threthewick. You must join my Society of Engineers, which I plan on launching soon. It will be an honour to have you join us. I'll see what I can do about your patent for your other invention — what's it called?"

"A Two-Wheeler."

"Right. I have considerable influence there, but if things get stuck at court, my hands are tied. There are more powerful men who can pull strings."

"Morley?" Philip gnashed his teeth.

"Your grandfather hasn't been seen in the House of Lords the last few decades. Can't imagine him having any say in the matter. I was thinking of someone else."

"Who would that be?"

The earl dropped the mechanical pencil into his hands. "The Duke of Ashmore."

PHILIP RETURNED WITH A WHIRLING MIND TO ROSETHISTLE Cottage.

He saw a light burning in the parlour room.

"Miss Weston! What are you doing up so late?"

She rose from the armchair. The candlelight cast shadows on her face. "I wanted to wait for you to ask: how did it go?" She looked very pretty in a simple blue gown that matched her eyes and the pink flush on her cheeks.

He tugged at his neckcloth. A man couldn't breathe in these damnable things. "Strange." He pulled the cloth off his neck and took a liberated breath. "Very strange."

He crumpled the cravat into a ball, threw it on the table,

dropped into a chair and motioned for her to sit. After a moment's hesitation, she sat on the edge of the chair.

"Strange," she repeated. "Is that good or bad?"

He reflected. To be fair, they hadn't been awful towards him. "They were surprisingly accepting of me. They were very curious."

"Of course. The Earl of Threthewick has been somewhat of a mystery thereabouts. How was supper?"

Philip reflected. "The meat was bland and the soup too salty."

Arabella smiled, and a dimple formed in her cheek. "I meant in terms of handling the utensils, of course."

He shuddered. "A nightmare. I may have used the fish fork for the meat."

She chuckled. It was a low laugh that gurgled in her throat. "And your invention?"

He furrowed his brows. "I am not certain. The earl seemed rather bored with my explanation of the problem. He did like this, though." He pulled the propelling pencil out of his waistcoat.

"What is it?"

"What do you think?" He leaned forward, eager for her opinion.

She turned it in her slim fingers, clicked on the top and when her lips formed an "oh," he saw that she understood instantly what it was. "It's a writing device that you don't have to sharpen. It is brilliant."

He grinned at her. "Yes, it is. It's nothing monumental. Yet the earl was as fascinated as a child. But he did promise to help me."

"It looks like the effort you put into this was worth it. That is great news, Mr Merivale."

"Philip. Call me Philip." Dash it, that had just come out of his mouth. Suddenly he wanted nothing more in the world than to hear his name on her lips. His gaze fell on the gentle curve of her mouth.

Her eyes grew round.

"Say it," his voice was hoarse.

Her lips trembled. "Philip," she whispered.

"Arabella." He took a deep breath. "Arabella. I would like to kiss you."

CHAPTER 2 4

*P*art of her had known it would happen.

It had been in the air. A sizzling energy that surrounded them and drew them closer.

They'd risen simultaneously. With a quick intake of breath, she lifted her head. Slowly, very slowly, he bent his head and brushed his lips against hers. She felt the sweet warmth and softness of his lips, at first hesitating, then growing more insisting, demanding.

Something inside her melted and it felt right, oh, so right.

It wasn't enough. She wanted to get closer. He took her in his arms and deepened the kiss. His hands dug into her hair and held her nape.

This, Arabella thought. *This.*

This was so much better than the wet peck Mr Gabriel had given her, or the misaimed kiss that Lord Finlay had tried to steal.

She sighed against his lips.

Philip kissed her once, twice, three times. Then held her in his embrace, her head against his heart, which thudded comfortingly.

Suspended in time, Arabella fell into a dreamy, content state. She could've stayed like that forever.

I'm so in love with you.

He let her go and stared at her as if he saw her for the first time.

Dear sweet heaven. She must've said it out loud. She coloured fiercely.

The silence between them became unbearable.

"Philip?" To her dismay, her voice broke slightly.

"I'm — I'm—" He took a step back. He pulled both hands through his hair and held them clasped behind his neck. "What completely inappropriate behaviour on my part."

She swallowed hard, trying to manage a feeble answer. "Inappropriate? Or inevitable?"

He took a step back. "Jenny."

Arabella flinched. "Jenny?"

"My wife."

She took a sharp intake of breath as his words pierced her heart.

He hesitated, measuring her for a moment. Then he stood straight and pulled down his waistcoat. "I — I am — I — I didn't think. Pray accept my apologies. It will not happen again." He gave a stiff bow and left the room.

Arabella remained alone in the room, her blood pounding with humiliation. What on earth had just happened? She buried her face with her hands. Did she really just declare her love for Philip Merivale — and been rejected?

ARABELLA PASSED THE NEXT DAY IN A DAZE. THROUGHOUT THE entire morning, she heard him hammering like a wild man in the forge. It disturbed their lessons. In the end, she dismissed the children with an assignment and returned to her room.

She dropped onto her bed, exhausted. It was barely noontime.

She'd tossed and turned the entire night. Her entire body alternately burning with humiliation, then shivering with chills when she recalled his rejection.

There'd been an undeniable attraction from the very first. She hadn't been wrong about that. She'd enjoyed every minute of his company, and she thought it had been mutual. The way his eyes lit up every time they landed on her. The way he liked to tease her. How easily they talked. How comfortable they felt in each other's company.

She'd never admired a man more. She'd never loved a man more. Arabella swallowed, as she acknowledged her feelings. It was true. She loved him. She'd known it for a while. She refused to be ashamed of her feelings.

And he?

He'd been married. To this Jenny. The mother of his three children.

Arabella groaned. Of course. How could she have forgotten? The children still loved and missed their mother dearly. Evidently, so did he. He will deny his attraction to her because of Jenny. How dare she think she could live up to her memory?

A heavy sadness weighed itself around Arabella's heart.

Their kiss had been a mistake.

Her confession of love, a disaster. What would happen now? Could she ever face him again?

She knew what she had to do. Raw grief overwhelmed her.

Someone knocked on her door. Arabella jumped up, her heart beating wildly. Maybe it was Philip...She blew her nose and wiped her cheeks before opening the door with shaking hands.

"Mail," Peggy grumbled. She held several letters in her hand and held out a missive.

"For me?" Arabella took it, surprised. Who knew she was living here? It was addressed to Miss Weston.

"The rest's for Mr Merivale. Invitations flooding in like there is no tomorrow."

Arabella nodded. Of course. Now they had a glimpse of the earl, they'd all want to invite the future Duke of Morley. That was how things went.

She turned her letter in her hands and opened it.

It was from Morley. His spidery handwriting was difficult to decipher.

He wanted to know whether she could finally arrange a meeting between the children and himself. In secret. For now, he wanted Philip to have no knowledge of this.

Arabella scowled. This crafty old man. After she'd learned about Philip's side of the story, she couldn't, with good conscience, go ahead with their agreement. She decided to ignore the letter.

Fergus left that afternoon. They stood outside the cottage and watched him load his cart. Arabella was sorry to see the old man go.

He'd looked at her with those crafty eyes of his and bid her farewell. "God speed, Miss. Take good care of my brood." She nodded.

Philip stood, both hands in his pocket, watching as his children took a tearful farewell of their great-grandfather.

"I'll be back again before Christmas." Fergus promised. Then he flicked his whip, and the cart started rolling.

She felt bereft when he disappeared behind the curve. She shivered in the cold, blustery wind. The children scampered off. Without so much as looking at her, Philip turned to leave.

Wrapping her arms about herself, she said, "I would like to speak with you, Mr Merivale."

He winced, then nodded. "Of course, Miss Weston." The entire morning he'd avoided her, and even now he did not meet her eyes. She swallowed the despair in her throat.

"I was thinking it may be time for me to move on as well." She clenched her fingernails into her palms.

His eyes flew to her face. "No."

"It would be for the best. A governess and her employer can't — shouldn't —" Tears blinded her eyes as she choked up. "And your children. Your w–wife. You loved her very much. It's become awkward, wouldn't you agree?"

He looked down at his feet, with his hands in his pocket. "Joy is not my child."

Arabella looked at him, bewildered. "I don't understand."

"She — Jenny." Philip looked at his boot as if there was something fascinating in the dust. "I was on the continent when she got pregnant. Basic mathematics."

Arabella's lips formed into a soundless O.

"Jenny wanted to marry the earl, not the blacksmith. She thought she could work me round, and sooner or later we'd be living in the grand mansion. She wanted to be a duchess. I wanted to dig my hands in ash and soot and trod in my grandfather's footsteps. And invent." From his feet, he looked up at the sky with a frown. "I thought I was so in love with her. But from the very first day it was a mismatch. But then Katy came and then Robin, and I didn't do so badly in the city. I could afford to buy her the lace and ribbons she wanted, the bonnets — and all those things." He shuffled again. "But we never stopped fighting. It got so bad. I enlist-ed." He looked straight into her face. "What Granda said was true. I fairly ran away from my family to war. Just to get away from her. Katy and Robin, they were so little. I deserted them."

"You did what you thought was best," Arabella whispered.

"He was some lord or other." Philip barked a short laugh. "Joy's father. A popinjay. She must have met him through Morley. She lived here at Thornton with the children while I was on the continent, even though she knew I was against it. Robin doesn't remember that time; Katy, barely. The irony is that after Jenny got pregnant by that popinjay, he enlisted, too. He didn't last a week."

"He fell?"

"Quatre Bras." Philip was lost in his memory. "Shortly after, Jenny died in childbirth."

Little Joy. That bright, cheerful little girl with blonde curls, like a doll.

"Joy is the apple of my eye. She is mine." Philip turned to her with a fierceness that took her aback. "I loved her from the minute she was born. She is a Merivale through and through. She is my child as much as Robin and Katy are."

Arabella felt moisture in her eyes. "She is so lucky to have you in her life."

"I have vowed to protect her as much as Robin and Katy. I don't want her to know the truth, but God help me, one day I will have to tell her. She has other family out there, probably. But I will make sure we will always be her true family."

"You couldn't be a better father."

"I try. I have made so many mistakes. Like yesterday." A rueful expression crossed his face. "I couldn't help but kiss you. But you are my children's governess. I am not going to be one of those employers who maul those in their employ. It is despicable behaviour."

Arabella swallowed. Ah. This is where the matter stood.

"Of course. I am just the governess, after all." Her voice sounded wooden to her ears.

"Arabella." His face hardened. "There is something else I want you to understand. I've been married once. It was a disaster. I take full responsibility for it. I have sworn I won't do it again."

"Do what?" she whispered.

"Love. Marriage. It works for others, but not for me." His eyes burned into hers. "Do you understand?"

Something in her died.

Arabella wrapped her arms around her mid-section. "I, um. I didn't really mean what I said yesterday. It was a spontaneous reaction to the, er, romance of the moment." She flushed miserably as she lied.

"Spontaneous reaction." She saw his Adam's apple twitch in his throat as he swallowed. "Naturally. Seen in this light …" He moved his lips, searching for words.

"We were both giddy with your success yesterday and got carried away." Arabella lifted her chin. Her bearing was stiff and proud, hiding the turmoil inside. "Shall we say that is all there is to it? And forget the entire episode?"

"That seems to be the best course of action," he mumbled. "You are right. It is best if you seek other employment. If you want, I can help you with that. But Miss Weston. Could you postpone that for a fortnight?" His eyes were sad and pleading.

She almost choked on the clump in her throat as she replied, "I think the sooner I leave, the better."

"I do need your assistance for another fortnight."

Arabella's shoulders slumped. Two more weeks of staying with the Merivale household, dragging out the inevitable end. It was going to be torture.

"It is because we are to go to London. I need your help with the children." He dragged his hair back with both hands in a motion that she'd grown to love.

"London."

He nodded. "I need to settle some business there, personally."

Arabella struggled with herself, then sighed. "Very well. A fortnight, you said?"

He nodded. "We will leave in two days."

CHAPTER 25

The coach Philip had hired to take them to London was neither comfortable nor swift. Arabella was used to her brother's well-sprung and elegant carriages, with seats covered in velvet. A second carriage with the ducal crest and flanked by outriders usually carried the luggage. Their luggage now was partially stowed away under their seats, taking away precious leg space. They'd stayed in two rough, dingy inns, but she'd gratefully accepted the hearty and simple meals she was given.

The coach plodded down the road and jolted her against the door. The seat was hard, and the edge cut into the hollow of her knees. She held the sleeping Joy, who drooled over her arm. Her shoulder felt stiff and cramped from accommodating Katy's head. Robin and his father sat across from her. Unable to sit still, Robin kicked his legs into hers with regularity, until he, too, dropped asleep. His father had pulled his bulging hat over his eyes and leaned back with crossed arms in the farthest corner. He'd been sleeping ever since.

Her heart ached every time she looked at his reclining figure. Philip had been as amiable as always, but also withdrawn and polite. Gone was the cheerful, teasing man she'd fallen in love with.

A hot wave of misery flooded through her. She'd been happy with them. She'd been doing so well. Then she'd gone and ruined it all by kissing Philip and telling him she loved him.

How stupid could one get?

Her days with the family were numbered. Then what? She couldn't imagine working as a governess elsewhere.

Return to her brother?

Arabella chewed on her bottom lip. He'd be furious and concerned. Having tragically lost his twin brother before she was born, she could understand why Henry was so overprotective of her. But it had stifled her.

She'd been determined to break out of the chains she'd been shackled to through mere birth. She wanted to carve her own life.

And then she'd gone and ruined it all.

What should she do now?

She thought of Miss Hilversham's Seminary in Bath. Would Miss Hilversham take her in? Arabella sighed. It was unlikely.

The smell of rust, smog, and sewer wafted through the carriage. They were approaching London.

Before he'd returned to Scotland, Fergus had gone ahead and rented a house for them, South of the River in Lambeth, complete with a maid. It was an area of London that Arabella hardly ever frequented. Several years ago, she'd visited the Royal Asylum for Female Orphans, which was located nearby, but that was about it. The coach drew up in front of a narrow sandstone–coloured house. Maggie, the maid, had been expecting them and showed her a small, clean room. Arabella took off her bonnet and rubbed her eyes tiredly.

"Mr Merivale wants to leave right away," Maggie informed her. "He'd like you to accompany them."

"Very well." She set the squashed straw bonnet on her head again.

Philip paced the hallway. "I need to get my business out of the way, the sooner the better."

"Very well, sir."

He threw her an odd look. "Good. Fine." Why did he keep looking at her?

"Are you well, Miss Weston?"

She clasped her hands tightly. "I am very well, sir."

"Fine, fine," Philip said with false heartiness. "Let us go, then. The children will join us. An outing in the park will do them good."

"Where are we going?"

"We are taking a walk in Hyde Park," Philip announced. "I thought the children could run in the park and stretch their legs, while I get my business done. I need to talk to the Duke of Ashmore. He lives in Grosvenor Square."

Arabella dropped her reticule. Philip stepped through the door and surveyed the street.

"Why do you want to talk to the Duke of Ashmore?" She caught up with him, breathless.

"He's the patron Winchester talked about. Apparently, he is immensely powerful and influential. He can pull some strings for me. God knows I detest having to do this, but things have gone so far that it is the only recourse open to me. If Ashmore has influence, I will take it."

"But — but." Arabella's mind was in a whirl. Now was the time to tell him she was Ashmore's sister. But he was already striding purposefully down the street, with Katy on one arm and Joy on the other.

"Mr Merivale. I need to tell you something." Arabella moistened her lips.

"Yes?" He looked distracted.

"Papa, can we go to Gunter's for ices afterwards?" Katy interjected.

"There's strawberry ice, lemon ice, vanilla ice…" Joy chanted as she hopped next to them.

"Can we, Papa, can we?"

"Oh yes, let's!" Katy and Robin talked simultaneously.

"Very well." Philip looked harassed. "What did you want to tell me, Arab — I mean, Miss Weston?"

"Do you also want ices, Miss Weston?" chattered Katy as she skipped along.

"I —" she swallowed. "Ices will be nice."

"Watch the carriages," Philip warned Robin and pulled him back by the collar.

Arabella followed them with a sinking feeling.

THE CHILDREN RAN IN THE PARK. JOY HAD TAKEN ALONG HER stick and hoop, whereas Robin pestered them about the balloon ascent that had taken place in Hyde Park at the jubilee celebration in eighteen-fourteen. He was clutching a roll of paper that he fervently refused to give up. Upon asking him what it was, he said with a sly smile that it was a big secret.

Arabella was glad of the big rim of the straw bonnet. She'd already seen more than one person who'd know her as Lady Arabella Astley. She hoped that with her threadbare bonnet and her plain dark brown dress she looked like a typical governess, and no one would pay her much notice. So far, it seemed to work. With some luck she could stay in the park with the children while Philip conducted his business with her brother. But why wasn't he leaving already? And why was he ushering them all across the street towards Grosvenor Square? He was busy explaining the mechanism of a steam engine to Robin as he strode quickly down the street.

"Sir, don't you want the children to play the park while you make your call?" Arabella asked breathlessly as she tried to keep up with him.

"You can wait for me on the bench on the square. Ah, it's here," Philip came to a full stop in front of a grand town-house that was very familiar to Arabella. She stared at it as if it were a dream. Philip rubbed his nose. "I had no idea he lived so close. Since we're already here, I'll talk to the fellow right away. There is no point in drawing things out." He started up the stairs.

"I will wait here with the children," Arabella said hastily. "Or you know what, why don't we return to the park while your father talks to the duke?" The further away they were, the better. She attempted to usher the children down the road.

"But we've already been at the park," Joy complained. "I'm tired and hungry and want to rest." She set her mouth in a stubborn line. "Besides, Papa said we could have ices."

"We can have ices afterwards." Arabella tried to coax her on. To no avail.

Joy threw a full-fledged tantrum in the middle of the street, right in front of the Ashmore residence.

Just at that moment, the door of the mansion opened, and a whirlwind emerged. It stopped on the top of the stairs shortly before an astonished Mr Merivale.

"Arabella!" a voice shrieked.

Arabella found herself engulfed in her sister-in-law's embrace.

Lucy. She was a slim woman with unruly brown curls and lively grey eyes, dressed in a walking dress of the latest fashion.

"I was about to go out with Henry, and would you know

it, here you are!" She engulfed Arabella in another tight hug. "I knew you'd return! I kept telling Henry, but he wouldn't believe me. He had to go and send out Bow Street Runners and it took me a devil of a time to convince him not to go dashing out himself, looking for you. Can you imagine? Bow Street Runners! But look at you! You look good and healthy and brown, and that is all that matters. Where have you been? Who's been screeching like a banshee? And who is he?" Lucy looked at Philip curiously. He'd taken a step back, and the children were watching with open mouths. Joy had mercifully stopped screeching.

Philip turned to Arabella. "Would you care to explain what is going on, Miss Weston?"

Lucy's eyes grew round. "Miss Weston? As in the name of our English teacher in school?"

"Judging from your expression of astonishment, ma'am, I surmise that this is not our governess' real name." His face darkened.

"Governess?" Lucy clasped her hand over her mouth. "You didn't!"

"It's — it's complicated." Arabella wanted to sit down on the stairs and weep.

Lucy pulled her aside. "Henry's coming out any minute. He's —"

"Henry's already here." A cool, male voice intruded. An impossibly tall, elegantly clad gentleman stood in the doorway and surveyed the scene. Ash, as Arabella fondly called him. There were lines of worry around his eyes which hadn't been there before. Arabella felt a pang of remorse. He'd worried about her. He'd sent out Bow Street Runners for her. A sob caught in her throat.

Ash's eyes rested on her. "Arabella." An infinitesimal shadow of relief crossed his face before he narrowed his eyes to grey slits of iron as he took in Philip and the children. "What, pray, is going on, here?" he asked quietly.

Arabella, who'd been about to throw herself at him, froze. She recognised that voice. He only spoke like that when he was very, very furious.

"My name is Philip Merivale." Philip scowled. "Who the devil are you?"

Ash threw an annihilating look at Philip.

Lucy drew his arm into hers.

"This is my husband Henry Astley, the Duke of Ashmore. Lady Arabella's brother."

"*Y*ou're the Duke of Ashmore's sister?" Philip's head snapped towards her.

Arabella dropped her head. "I am so sorry. I wanted to tell you, but —"

Philip struggled for something coherent to say. He felt like he was about to have an apoplexy on the street.

"Papa?" Katy tugged on his arm. She looked fearfully from one person to another.

He pulled himself together. "I think we just discovered your governess, here, is the Duke of Ashmore's sister." He tried to say so in a light, jovial tone, as if it wasn't even worth mentioning, but a streak of fury jolted through him. She'd told him she was an impoverished daughter of a baron, confound it, and that she'd fallen on hard times. He'd never believed her and guessed that she was the daughter of an earl, or a marquess. It turns out she's the sister of that powerful patron he was supposed to charm. A bloody duke. That was a different story altogether and entirely intolerable.

Why were the women in his life consistently lying and deceiving him? Even Katy had gone behind his back to hire the governess. Who now turned out to be a blasted duke's sister.

Plague and pest —

"Merivale. We can, of course, continue to converse in the streets if you prefer, or we can go inside and gather in the drawing room like reasonable, civilised people." The duke's cold voice left no doubt as to which it was going to be.

His tone raised Philip's hackles. He threw him a look of hostility. Bah, they were all the same. A breed of people thinking they were superior to everyone else. This one wasn't going to be any exception.

The duke surveyed the children. "These are yours?"

"Katy, Robin, and Joy," Philip bit out. The three stared at the duke, terrified.

"Wonderful! I was about to go out shopping, I need a new hat, you know, but this of course tops everything." Lucy pulled Arabella up the stairs. "Oh, to find you on our immediate doorstep! With such adorable children, too. Didn't I tell you only this morning not to worry, Henry? Arabella's just fine. Aren't you?" She patted her arm. "Come inside, everyone, come inside. I will ring for some tea." Lucy smiled warmly at Philip and held out a hand to little Joy, who, after a moment's hesitation, took it.

"I have a mouse," she informed Lucy. "In my pocket."

"That's splendid, my darling. You have to tell me all about her."

"It's a he. His name is Minimus."

"What a fabulous name for a mouse! Do you think Minimus wants to eat ices in the nursery?"

Katy and Robin gasped. "Ices! Like they serve at Gunter's?" Katy asked.

"Better," Lucy winked at her.

Joy made a thoughtful face. "Minimus likes strawberry ice."

"Strawberry ice it is, then. Mrs Willow?" An elderly matron with a gleaming white cap appeared.

"Yes, Your Grace?"

Philip blinked, when he realised the whirlwind of a girl who seduced his children with ices must be the duchess. She definitely did not fit his image of what a duchess ought to look like.

"If the children would like to follow me?" Mrs Willow smiled at the children.

Three pairs of heads turned to Philip.

He swallowed. Then nodded. It was probably best not to have them witness the ensuing scene.

The children followed Mrs Willow to the nursery, while Lucy ushered them into a blue and gold drawing room and rang a bell.

"I am so glad you decided to return," he heard her whisper to Arabella.

"You must tell me all about your adventures."

"Indeed." The duke's eyes nailed him down. "An explanation is in order."

Philip tugged at his blasted neckcloth. His prospects of getting the duke's patronage for his inventions went down the river.

As soon as the footman had brought in the tea tray and left, the duke crashed down on him.

"Merivale." The duke said heavily. "Did you compromise my sister?"

THE WORDS HUNG IN THE AIR FOR AN AWFUL MOMENT. THEN everyone talked at the same time.

"The devil! Of course I didn't —"

"Henry!"

"How *awful* of you, Ash!" Arabella felt like bursting into tears.

"Then what, if you please, is the precise nature of your relationship to my sister?"

Philip set down his teacup so hard it must've cracked. He jumped up. "The precise nature of my relationship to your sister, Your *Grace*," he hissed, "is that she has, in gross deception which she has maintained these past two months, pretended to be a governess in my household. She claimed to be a baron's daughter who'd fallen upon hard times." A deep red flush spread over his face and his eyes turned into bright hard chinks of emerald.

"A governess!" Her brother glared at him as if that were his fault. "Good heavens. And you didn't immediately realise that she dished you up a bag of Banbury tales?"

"Of course, I realised it, Your Grace," Philip bit out and turned an even darker shade of puce. "But I most certainly did not realise she was your sister. Contrary to what you may think, it's not as though that particular identity is written on her forehead."

Ashmore's expression seemed to say he was entirely wrong and that the identity of an Ashmore was always evident.

Philip matched his glare with such open antagonism that Arabella feared the two were but a minute away from throwing themselves at each other.

"And what, exactly, did you think of doing with my sister in London?" The duke asked softly.

"We're here because — dash it all, I don't need to explain myself to you!" Philip finally exploded.

"Considering the lady in question is my sister, you certainly must explain yourself to me." Ashmore had never been as pompous.

"Boys, don't fight," Lucy's soothing tones intervened. "I'm

sure Arabella has a valid explanation as to why she thought she needed some time on her own to be a governess. In fact, if you come and think about it, it makes perfect sense. Governessing is the only respectable job a woman can have, and I am certain Arabella did a fantastic job of it."

"I am still here, you know." Arabella's head ached.

"I can assure you I'd never have hired your sister had I known she was your sister! I never wanted a blasted governess in the first place. We Merivales can do without governesses."

The duke frowned. "Merivale. Merivale. The name sounds deucedly familiar. Are you —"

"I'm a blacksmith." Philip jutted his chin out. "Have been and always will be. Inventor too."

"Why does a blacksmith need a governess?" Ashmore lifted an eyebrow.

"Why? What's it to you? Why aren't blacksmith's children allowed to have an education as much as a duke's?" Philip sounded like he contradicted himself just to be able to contradict the duke.

"My dear fellow, that's not the issue at hand. Whatever reasons my sister has for parading about as a governess —"

Arabella stood up, walked to the coffee table, picked up the vase with the carnations in it, and smashed it on the ground. "Will you all stop talking about me as though I'm a piece of furniture incapable of thinking and speaking?" she shouted.

For the first time in twenty-two years, Lady Arabella finally spoke up. It felt liberating.

She took advantage of the astonished silence. She turned to her brother. "Ash, you know I love you. But why can't you understand you are stifling me with all this overprotective-ness? I can't take a step without you hovering over me! I know I have a duty to our name and lineage, I know of it, as much as you. But why can't you see I want to make my own decisions? Do something useful with my life. Yes, I went to Cornwall on a whim, answering an advertisement which his daughter placed, because I wanted to. I worked as a governess. I wanted to prove to myself that I could do this. It isn't shameful. And you, Lucy," she turned to her friend and took her hands, "stop fighting my battles for me. I know you mean well, but you've got to let me make my own mistakes." Lucy teared up and nodded.

"And you, Mr Merivale." Arabella almost choked. "I apologise sincerely for having misled you so grossly, it wasn't done with malicious intent. Never so."

Philip nodded curtly and blinked fast. "Apology accepted."

"Ash, they were wonderful to me. Nothing inappropriate ever happened." Better not tell him about swimming in the lake in her petticoat. Or living unchaperoned with him under the roof. Or that kiss...She avoided Philip's eyes. "The Merivales were always gracious, kind and — w–w– welcoming." She finally burst into tears.

Ash stepped up and took her in his arms.

Lucy first gave a wobbly smile, then cried right along with her.

Philip shifted from one foot to the other, then into a water puddle left by the broken vase, and looked alternately at the ceiling, the window, and the broken shards on the floor.

The door opened and the butler entered.

"Your Grace."

Ashmore released Arabella. His own eyes were red.

"The Duke of Morley is here."

"The devil," breathed Philip.

188

CHAPTER 27

"*M*orely?" Ashmore's brows cleared as he understood. Turning to the butler, he said, "The complete name, Howard, if you please."

"His Grace George Merivale, the Duke of Morley," the butler announced.

The old man hobbled into the room. He broke into a huge smile when he saw Philip.

"My grandson." Lifting his cane, he spread his arms.

Philip backed off and fully stepped into the water puddle. "I am not your grandson."

Ashmore lifted an eyebrow. "Merivale. I should have realised sooner."

The old duke nodded. "My son was Edward Merivale." He waved a gnarly hand at Philip. "This is Philip Merivale, the Earl of Threthewick. My grandson." There was pride in his voice.

"I am not his grandson," Philip repeated. "I am not an earl. I am a blacksmith." He jutted out his chin and glared at them.

"Of course you are." Lucy patted his arm.

"No doubt you will make up your mind in good time as

to who you are," Ashmore informed him. A muscle twitched in his cheek, which was the only indication he was amused.

"Psahw. He always says that." The old man dropped into an armchair. He looked at Lucy. "You must be the duchess." In the general upheaval of his arrival, they'd forgotten about formal introductions.

His eyes fell on Arabella, who skulked in a corner and his face brightened. "Lady Arabella. What joy to see you again."

Arabella closed both eyes. She physically felt the shock that went through Philip as he whirled to look at her.

"What? You two know each other?" He looked from one person to the other.

"But of course. We had a nice afternoon tea in Thornton Hall on her day off. I must say, I was disappointed you never replied to my missive. But then in a roundabout way you did end up helping me reunite with my grandson. I simply followed you here to London, you see."

Philip's blood drained from his face.

"Lady Arabella was so kind as to arrange a meeting between us." Turning to Ashmore, he said, "You must forgive me that I drag you into this family affair. Your sister has been most helpful."

"I am keen to learn in what way Arabella helped reunite you with your grandson." Ashmore sat down and crossed his legs.

"You are doing it again, Ash." Arabella set her lips in a mulish line.

"What?" Her brother knitted his brows.

"Speaking as though I am not in the room." Her nerves were close to snapping.

"Then tell us, Miss Weston." Philip burst forth. "I mean, Lady Arabella. How did you come to know Morley and what, exactly, was your role in getting him here?" Philip crossed his arms and there was an expression in his eyes that made her gulp.

"It is as the duke says. We had tea and he asked me to..." she groped for the right term, as 'spy' didn't seem like a good choice.

"Yes?"

"Be an intermediary between you two. At that time, I thought it was a good idea."

With eyes as hard as steel, Philip said, "You are in league with him. Like I suspected from the very first."

Arabella wanted to deny it, but a streak of guilt flashed through her. "It's not like you think. It really isn't."

A muscle jumped in Philip's cheek. "You met with him behind my back even though you knew how I'd felt about him. You were going to help him kidnap my children."

"No!" Arabella couldn't believe he just uttered these words. "How can you even think that!" Least of all say it out loud, in front of her brother, Lucy and his grandfather.

"I knew there was something off from the first time we met. The way you talk, the way you carry yourself. I swallowed the bag of moonshine that you'd dished me up. Of course, you'd be on his side. I should've trusted my instincts."

"Mind your words, Threthewick, you are talking to my sister." Ashmore's ice-cold voice cut into their conversation.

Arabella felt a sword slash through her heart. "You're wrong. I am sorry I deceived you, but I really thought at the time my identity didn't matter. I only wanted the best for you and the children." Her voice thickened with tears.

Philip stemmed his hands against his hips, looked at the ceiling with a bitter smile and shook his head.

"That's what everyone says. That's what he says." He jerked his chin in the direction of Morley, who was listening raptly. "Because it's in my best interest, he thought it was right to take me away from my mother. He killed her."

Lucy gasped.

"Watch yourself. You are under my roof and I will not have my guests accused of murder," Ashmore's voice slashed.

Philip ignored him. "I am going to fetch my children." He strode towards the door. "Miss Weston." He did not meet her eyes. "You are dismissed as governess."

He stalked out of the room.

This was the third time he'd dismissed her. It would be the last time.

Arabella wanted to run after him but caught herself in time. He thought her complicit in a ploy to kidnap his children. How could he? How *dare* he?

"You must forgive him. He has the Morley temper," the old man said as he helped himself to a pinch of snuff from a small silver box. He offered it to Ashmore, who shook his head impatiently. "But he is right on one account." He closed the box with a flick and sighed. "I did kill his mother." A clock ticked in the shocked silence.

"No doubt you will tell us the story in your own time, Duke," Ashmore drawled, after the moment dragged out.

"Wait. Let me order some more tea." Lucy scrambled up and rang the bell. "For fortification." The footman brought in a tea tray. Lucy poured tea and handed a cup to the old duke.

His hand shook as he lifted the cup. He took a sip and sighed. "Ah, there is nothing like a good cup of strong tea to lift one's spirits."

"Something tells me they are about to get depressed again," Lucy whispered to Arabella.

Ashmore steepled his fingers. "Morley?"

The old man cleared his throat. "My son, Edward, married a laundry maid. A gutter rat. I was livid. He did it only to spite me."

"They might've fallen in love?" Lucy propped her elbows on her knees, leaning forward.

"Love! Pshaw."

"It does happen." She looked fondly at Ashmore, who softened and smiled, transforming his entire being.

"No. He did it because he knew it was the only way to get back at me."

"Get back at you for what?" Arabella asked.

Morley told them the whole story. At the end, he sighed. "Admittedly, I may have been too harsh on the boy. He was too sensitive, and the only way to fix that was to toughen him up."

"By sending a child out at night and shooting guns over his head?" Arabella interjected.

"He didn't!" Lucy exclaimed.

"Aside from your hideous notions regarding child-rearing, let us get to the heart of the matter. Did you kill Threthewick's mother?" Ashmore asked.

The duke sighed. "She came to fetch her son and offered an exchange that I found unreasonable. We quarrelled. Unfortunately, we happened to be at the top of the stairs in my house, and because she was overly upset, she stumbled when she left. She fell down the stairs and broke her neck." He lowered his head. "She was with child."

Lucy covered her mouth with her hands.

"So, it was an accident." Ashmore narrowed his eyes.

The duke nodded. "If I'd shown her the courtesy a father-in-law commonly shows his daughter-in-law and invited her into the drawing room, this might have been prevented." He sat up straight. "I take responsibility. Her unfortunate demise was entirely my fault." Stifling silence filled the room.

"But now, what? He doesn't acknowledge you. Don't you think you should respect that?" Lucy asked.

"Look at me. My time is nearly up. I would like to mend my relationship with my grandson and my enchanting great-grandchildren in the little time that's left. But you may be right, Duchess." Sighing, he pulled himself up on his cane, "It seems to be an entirely futile endeavour."

He hobbled to the door, stopped and turned to Arabella. "I would've liked to have you as my granddaughter-in-law. Whatever the term is. I am truly getting too old. Ashmore. Duchess." He nodded at them and left.

Ashmore turned to Arabella with a frown. "Is there something you want to tell me?"

Arabella shook her head so hard the pins in her hair nearly shot across the room. "No. Definitely not."

Lucy threw Ashmore a warning look. "Shall we go visit Isolde in the nursery?"

Arabella jumped up. "Oh yes, let's. I haven't seen her in such a long time. How she must've grown!"

"Growing like there is no tomorrow! And teething like something terrible." Lucy pulled her out of the room.

Looking back, Arabella saw her brother lean back in the fauteuil, frowning, as he processed this morning's events.

Her own heart needed sorting out as well.

It throbbed dully.

CHAPTER 2 8

"*P*apa, Robin is missing," Katy said breathlessly, running into her father's study of the London townhouse.

Philip, who'd been busily working on his newest invention, as he told himself, but in reality had been staring out of the window, looked up briefly. "He's probably with the boys next door showing them his newest paper model."

Robin had discovered the art of folding wings out of paper, so it flew, and he'd spent an ungodly amount of paper trying to fold the right model.

"He isn't. I just checked." Katy pushed her strands of hair out of her face, exasperated. "Oh, why can't Miss Weston be here? Things were so much easier when I didn't have to babysit the little ones." She'd been in a sulk since he'd dismissed Miss Weston earlier that day.

He ground his teeth. "Don't mention her name again, ever."

"But, Papa. It really isn't her fault that she's a duke's sister." She shook her head. "You also didn't bother to tell her you were a duke's grandson. Anyway, what does it matter?"

She was right. He felt ashamed his fourteen–year–old daughter was being more adult in this situation than he.

But he simply couldn't get over this feeling of betrayal. Going behind his back, dealing with his grandfather. Having tea with him in secret at Thornton Hall. Like Jenny.

Very well, so not quite as bad as Jenny. She hadn't said a vow, had she? They weren't married after all. And she hadn't been unfaithful. So why did it feel like she was? He pulled his thumb over his metallic writing device, forgetting it wasn't a quill, and ripped his skin open. "Ow." A drop of blood oozed out. He stuck it in his mouth.

He'd been brooding over Arabella the entire day. Confound it, he'd been thinking about her since the minute he'd left the ducal townhouse.

If he was going to be honest with himself, he'd have to admit he'd thought of her every single minute since the moment they'd met. It was almost as if she'd taken possession of his heart and soul.

He dropped his pen.

No, his thoughts weren't going there. Where was he, and what was he supposed to be doing, again? He shuffled amongst his sheets hectically and stared sightlessly at his design.

"Papa?" Katy was still there, fidgeting.

"Oh. Robin." Guilt flashed through him. He'd been so absorbed in his own problems that he'd forgotten about his children. "The library, maybe?"

"No. It's evening. It's already closed." Katy took a big breath. "Do you think — do you think *he* took him?" A coldness seeped into his heart.

He wouldn't. Not after today.

Would he?

Philip jumped up. "I'll go back to the duke's house. Maybe he's returned there. Ices and all that." When Philip had barged into the nursery to hustle his children home, Robin had protested vehemently, for he'd barely begun to eat his ices. It had taken him a considerable amount of persuasion to leave without Miss Weston.

"You're right." Katy brightened. "He may have returned to talk to Miss Weston."

Philip pulled on his jacket. "Watch Joy for me. I'll be back with Robin shortly."

Hopefully.

But Robin wasn't at the Ashmore residence.

The butler, confound him, merely shook his head, with half-closed eyes. "No, my lord. The child hasn't been here since you left this afternoon. I recall he went with you."

Philip blinked, irritated, at the 'my lord'. "It can't be. Check again."

"Mr Merivale?" There she stood. The woman he'd thought about all day. Oddly enough, she appeared prettier than he'd remembered. "Whatever is the matter?" A faint rosy blush tinted her cheeks.

He tore the hat off his head and stuttered, remembering that they hadn't parted on the best of terms. Then he pulled himself together. This was about his son. "Robin. He's disappeared. If he's not here, then there is only one other place where he would be."

She looked at him coldly. "You are not implying I have had anything to do with that, are you, Mr Merivale?" She'd never appeared haughtier.

Now it was his turn to blush. "I — er — I. No. I apologise for my previous words. They were hastily spoken. I didn't think." He realised he'd been an arse. He folded the hat in his hands. Their eyes met.

"The Duke of Morley." She frowned. "Somehow, after

everything that's happened, I don't think he would kidnap Robin."

Philip sighed. "You don't know him. But you are right. It would be odd."

She dropped her head. "No. I don't. But let me come with you." He paused. Then nodded tersely.

"I will be ready shortly."

Arabella reappeared soon after, wearing a pale blue pelisse, accompanied by a maid.

ROBIN WASN'T AT THE DUKE OF MORLEY'S HOUSE, EITHER. THE butler's expression of cluelessness had been so authentic, that there was no doubt the boy was not there. Morley himself, the butler said, was indisposed. But at Philip's insistence, the butler went up and returned with Morley, who looked grey.

"Robin is not here, son," he said. "You have to believe me." The old man looked truly distressed.

Philip stared at him.

Arabella tugged at his sleeve. "I think he is telling the truth," she said gently.

"God knows you have no cause to trust me. But I am indeed speaking the truth. The boy is not with me, nor have I any hand in his disappearance." He frowned. "In fact, this is worrisome. If you like, I can help find him. I have connections with the Bow Street Runners."

Philip felt the blood drain from his face. "It hasn't come thus far."

The duke summoned the butler. "If he is not in his usual places, I strongly suggest we hire the Bow Street Runners. Let me do that for you." The duke placed a gnarly hand on his arm.

Philip looked at it. Then he nodded.

Morley looked relieved. "In the meantime, continue looking. I will notify you if there is news."

Philip and Arabella left the duke's home. "I blame myself," Philip said. "I should've given him more attention. Where could he have gone?"

"Have you checked Hyde Park? He's been talking about the balloons, so maybe he wanted to see the place where the last ascent was." Arabella suggested.

Philip's face brightened. "Of course! Let us go there right away." But he wasn't at the park.

With every minute that passed that Robin wasn't found, Philip's panic grew. They returned to his grandfather's house, where the butler informed them that the Bow Street Runners were already scouring the streets.

Morley joined them in the drawing room, wearing an embroidered banyan. The worry in his eyes seemed authentic.

"What is taking them so long to return with news?" he muttered and hobbled outside to consult with his butler.

Philip collapsed in an armchair.

Arabella sat next to him. "They will find him," she said in a soothing voice.

He uttered a hollow laugh. "Ironic that I am applying to my grandfather, of all people, for help."

Arabella hesitated before she said. "I understand what you went through as a child was a terrible experience for you. There is no excuse for that." She hesitated before she continued. "He told us the story of how your mother died. It seems to have been an accident. He admitted to having been responsible and took the blame. I also had the impression your grandfather, at least in part, seems to feel some regret for his actions, for the way he has treated you and your mother. He seems sincere in wanting to make amends."

Philip leaned his head against the armchair's upholstery

and closed his eyes wearily. "Maybe. I don't know. I don't care about what my grandfather feels or doesn't feel. I only care about my son." He opened his eyes and regarded Arabella. "Nothing matters to me more than my children. Nothing."

Lowering her head, she nodded. "Of course. It wouldn't be natural otherwise." Maybe he imagined it, but she seemed to wilt just a bit.

He pulled a hand through his thick hair. "I was unfair to you earlier. I made unfair accusations. For that I apologise. I always prided myself in being an even-tempered man." He pulled a wry smile. "I suppose I've got a temper, after all."

She acknowledged his apology with a nod and played with the golden teaspoon. The tea, untouched, had long gone cold.

"There is another idea that I have." She sat up straight. "How could I have been so foolish as not to think of this earlier?"

Philip looked at her with incomprehension. "What do you mean?"

"I think I know where Robin is." She got up.

"Where?"

Arabella took several steps to the door, turned and with a deep breath said, "Do you trust me?" There was something in her eyes that made him realise that his answer to this question mattered.

He floundered and flailed. "Um."

Not the right answer. Arabella seemed to think so, too. Her shoulders slumped as she turned away.

"Of course I do," he said a tad too quickly. "But what does this have to do with Robin?"

"Come with me," she said, putting on her bonnet.

"Where to?"

"To Whitehall."

Philip stopped in his tracks; thunderstruck. "The Home Office? What would he do there?"

"To talk to Lord Henry Addington."

"What, by Jove, would he want with Addington —" He broke off, as he understood. Then he slapped his forehead. "Of course."

His son had gone to see the Home Secretary to get his invention patented.

They found Robin slumped on a chair by the wall in a room with wood panelling. He clutched a roll of paper and looked tired.

"Papa!" He scrambled up when he saw them hurry into the room.

With shaking breath, Philip gathered him into a hug. "Robin. Thank God."

"Miss Weston!" The boy's face brightened as he looked over his father's shoulder. "Did you return to us?"

"Oh, Robin." Arabella shook her head. "What on earth has gotten into you, running away like that?"

"But I had to come here to make an appointment with the Home Secretary. It's for a patent, you see."

Philip didn't know whether to laugh, shout, or scold. He ended up dropping into the chair beside Robin and felt the full force of exhaustion roll over him like a deluge. "Robert Benjamin Merivale. You are grounded for the rest of your life."

The boy's face fell. "But starting only after I talk to the Home Secretary." That boy's stubbornness was nearly as strong as his own.

A harassed-looking clerk appeared in front of them. "Is this your boy? He has been waiting here the entire afternoon and won't go away. I told him well over ten times that Lord

Addington has all his appointment slots filled. He can't just show up here, wanting to talk to the Home Secretary. People need to make an appointment first. Some wait for nearly a year." He pursed his lips in disapproval and made a motion with his hands, as if they were vermin, and he wanted to shoo them out of the room.

Something in Philip snapped.

He stood up straight. "My name is Threthewick." His voice sounded cold and haughty. "The Earl of Threthewick. My grandfather —" his voice shook. "My grandfather is the Duke of Morley."

The earth didn't shake, the walls still stood, as Philip finally claimed his heritage. He felt something unfamiliar pulse through his veins: pride.

"I am Lady Arabella Astley. The Duke of Ashmore's sister," Arabella said in a cool voice. "I believe you will obtain his lordship an appointment with Addington within the minute."

The clerk's eyes widened. "Morley? Ashmore?" he gulped. "It will be but a second, my lord. My lady." He scuffled off.

Philip couldn't believe he had done that. He'd broken all his principles and used his grandfather's name. He didn't like that one bit. But, by Jove, if that was what would get him what he wanted, so be it.

"Brilliant," Robin said, delighted.

The clerk came scuttling back. "He will see you immediately." There were beads of sweat on his forehead.

Robin rushed forward, and Philip made a motion to follow him, when he noticed that Arabella lingered.

"I will say goodbye here," she said in a soft voice, her hands clasped in front of her. "You are close to realising your dreams." She looked at him for a moment.

There was something in her eyes, but he couldn't read it. Was it sadness? Regret?

"Goodbye, Mr Merivale. God speed." She turned to go.

His stomach knotted together as if an ice-cold stone had settled in it. He could call her back. Ask her to stay. Ask her to — what, exactly? His mind was fogged.

"Arabella." His voice broke as he said her name.

But she was already gone.

As he went to join his son and the Home Secretary in the office, he couldn't help but feel that he'd just lost something infinitely precious.

*A*rabella mourned.

If she could, she'd wear black weeds, but how would she explain that to her brother and to Lucy?

She was mourning the loss of a love that had never been. For she had no place in Philip Merivale's life. Oh yes, she'd pretended she'd been able to integrate into their lives, but it was all based on a lie. She'd thought she could reinvent herself by becoming Arabella Weston.

And deny her roots, her heritage. Her self.

But all she'd accomplished was that she'd been enchanted by a family that wasn't her own. She'd gotten her heart broken. She missed Katy, Robin, and Joy with a fierceness that frightened her.

Arabella dared not think of Philip.

The thought of having lost him sucked her into a black hole so deep, she feared she'd never emerge from it again.

"Do I need to call out Threthewick?" Ash had asked after casting one look at her stricken face. She knew that, despite his aloof behaviour, he worried about her.

"No," she choked.

Ash nodded and without a word took her in his arms, where she cried her heart out. "You just have to say the word, should you change your mind. I'll gladly whip him for you." He handed her his handkerchief.

"Ash?" she asked, after noisily blowing her nose.

"Yes, Bella?" he hadn't called her that since she was ten. The look of concern in his eyes almost made her burst into tears again.

"Don't fight my battles for me."

He looked searchingly in her face. Then he nodded. "If you really don't want me to, then I won't, little sister."

Arabella had returned with Ash and Lucy to Ashmore Hall. Life there seemed to continue as usual, but everything had changed.

She was no longer the same.

She supposed love tended to do that to people.

At least she'd proven to herself that she could support herself. She'd learned that working for a living could be satisfying. She learned how to swim. How to cook. How to teach.

But what would she do now? She could not, for the life of her, return to her previous frivolous life of embroideries, ton parties, and balls, where the biggest issue was catching a husband. She'd lost all interest in that life long ago.

"I know what I am going to do with my life," she announced to Lucy in the nursery one day. Lucy was in the process of changing Isolde's napkins. The nurse hovered in the background and wrung her hands, for how could a duchess change her baby's napkins?

"Splendid, Arabella." Lucy pinned the linen around the baby, who cooed. "Tell me."

"I am going to be a spinster."

Lucy shot her a quick glance. "Excellent. You are aware that means you'll be stuck with us for the rest of your life?"

She picked up the baby and settled her on her shoulder. "I wouldn't mind that in the least. Neither would Isolde. The only worry I'd have is you'd be dissatisfied living with us. How about becoming an eccentric and setting up your own household?"

A ghost of a smile flitted around Arabella's lips. "I've thought about it. I want to do something useful. I want to work."

"Ash will break out in hives, but I understand."

"Ash has promised to no longer interfere with my life."

"Yes, and unicorns fly."

"I really think he means it this time. I thought of talking to Miss Hilversham and supporting her seminary. And maybe building up my own school. Putting all my energy to the cause of female education."

"Oh Arabella, that is brilliant. You know Miss Hilversham will always welcome you with open arms — as a patroness. But she'll never hire you as a teacher."

"I know." Arabella bit her lip before saying, "My status is in the way. But maybe I can have an influence on what things are taught. Proper things. Like advanced natural sciences. And higher mathematics. Maybe even engineering... And maybe she'll let me talk to the students. On an occasional visit. And one day I can have my own school..." Her voice petered off.

Lucy nodded. "You have a plan. Do it. I will wholeheartedly support you, and surely Ash will, too. If that is what you want, if that is what you think will make you happy, then we will all support you."

"Yes. I am fairly certain that is what I want." She smiled at Lucy brightly and held out her hands for little Isolde, who gurgled at her aunt.

Her heart, however, said something else.

CHAPTER 30

"*P*apa, I wish Miss Weston were back with us."
Robin had thrown his quill down in frustration
and splattered ink over the table.

Philip sighed. He'd tried to spend the entire afternoon
teaching his children. Instead of returning to Cornwall,
Philip had decided to stay longer until they found a new
governess. They'd interviewed at least five applicants, but
none would do. One looked terrifying, with pinched mouth
and sunken cheeks and was unanimously rejected. One had
declared she didn't believe in reading stories to children,
because it unnecessarily incited one's imagination and had
frowned disapprovingly at Joy, who'd clung to her Mouse
book. One had burst into tears when Philip asked her why
she'd applied for the job, and another applicant was so old
she had difficulty climbing the steps up to the front door.
The last one had called Philip's inventions the work of the
devil and fled.

So, Philip had to resort to schooling his children himself,
like he'd done before, but somehow it wasn't the same. He
discovered he did not know many things Arabella had taught

them. He spoke neither Italian nor French well, so their language studies came to a halt. He was horrendously unmusical, so he'd scratched music lessons as well. He couldn't help Katy with her needlework and had no idea whether mauve or vermillion threads were better suited for flower petals. "Use both," he'd advised.

Katy pouted. "If Miss Weston were here —"

"I know, I know." Philip pulled his hair. "If Miss Weston were here, everything would be so much better, the quality of life would improve, the sun would come out, and the world would turn again."

The children nodded in agreement.

Robin sat up straight. "I know what you can do." He rushed to the door.

"Robert Benjamin Merivale, where do you think you are going?"

"To fetch Miss Weston back."

"Excellent, Robin. I'll come too." Katy jumped up.

"Me too!" Joy piped up.

"Sit." Philip's voice slashed through the room and was blithely ignored. "Robin, Katy, Joy! Be reasonable. Miss Weston really isn't Miss Weston."

"No. She isn't." Katy whirled at him. "Don't you see? Things could be so easy, Papa. But if you aren't going to do it, then we will." She set her mouth in a mulish line.

Philip raked his hand over his face. "I haven't the faintest idea what you are talking about."

The children exchanged looks. Robin rolled his eyes.

"Miss Weston is Lady Arabella," Katy said slowly. "She is the sister of a duke."

"So?" A similarly mulish look appeared on Philip's face. One need merely mention the word "duke" to set him off.

"You, Papa. Are. Going. To. Be. A. Duke." The words dropped in the room. Katy crossed her arms.

"Not if I can help it." Philip ground his teeth.

"But that's exactly it. You *can't* help it, Papa," Robin suddenly he seemed old beyond his years. "It's a fact. You know it. And I know it. And after you, *I* will be duke. And you know what?" He glared at his father. "I *want* to be a duke. There is nothing whatsoever you can do about it."

Philip opened his mouth to reply, to say something scathing, but there was indeed nothing, whatsoever, that he could say to counter that particular piece of fact. Because Robin, of course, was right.

Out of the mouths of babes.

"The Duke of Morley, our great-grandfather, has never tried to harm us." Katy piped in. "I know he tried to hurt you once, Papa. But he never tried to do that to Robin. Or me. I remember many years ago when you were at war and we visited him at Thornton Hall with Mama and you were so furious. He tried to be *kind* to us. It didn't come to him naturally, not like Granda, but he tried, you could see he really tried. You don't have to like him. But I think you're not being fair by not giving us the chance to get to know him. He is the only family we have left, other than Granda."

Robin nodded furiously.

Philip shook his head. "He is not family and he never will be. Whatever bonds we have is entirely biological. Forget the man. I will not let him claim you, put a finger on you and spoil you. And turn you into one of his creatures."

"But —"

"Enough, Katherine. Sit down and finish whatever you need to finish. We will not discuss this again. You are all grounded until further notice." The three children looked at him, startled. Philip never raised his voice.

He left the house and slammed the door shut.

Philip needed air. He needed space to breathe.

Night had fallen, and he walked swiftly down the street. Somewhere. Anywhere.

After half an hour of vigorous walking, he'd cooled off and regretted his words. His children were right. He was being stubborn and unreasonable.

But to get Miss Weston back? To see the shy smile in her blue eyes, how they lit up every time they fell on him. How she bent her blonde head over Joy, showing her how to draw letters. How she laughed with Robin and understood Katy, who was growing into womanhood.

It was a fact: the world had turned grey and lustreless since she'd left.

He'd lost his drive to invent. What was the point of it all anyway?

What did he want, confound it?

He wanted Arabella.

He sat down on a bank and stared into the darkness.

Then it hit him. It struck like lightning. The sun rose in the middle of the night as a golden glow of light engulfed him.

"I am such an oaf," he muttered, startling the lamplighter, who'd just refuelled the lamp next to his bank with oil. "I am such a tremendous, idiotic, brainless oaf."

How could he have fallen in love with her and never even noticed until now? He'd told Arabella he wouldn't love again. That love and marriage wasn't for him.

What tosh. When he'd been in love with her all along.

"I am an —"

"Aye, mister, said that a good three times already," the lamplighter grumbled as he climbed down from his ladder.

"What would you do, if you realised you loved a lady?" Philip asked, dazed.

"You askin' me?"

"If you please."

The man puffed up his breast. "I'd marry her."

Philip stared at the man.

"I am such an oaf," he said again. But this time he grinned. He got up, slapped the man's shoulder. "Thank you."

"Welcome," he grunted and shook his head. Philip sprinted back to his house.

First, he'd have to apologise to his children.

Then, he'd have to travel to Ashmore Hall. To ask Arabella to marry him.

In front of his house, he found a carriage with a familiar ducal crest. The Duke of Morley! What did he want now?

He bound up the stairs, taking two at a time. He found the children in the drawing room, sitting on one side at the table, staring at a man who sat at the other side.

"Who're you?" Philip demanded. He took in the man's blue and gold livery.

The footman jumped up. "My lord," he stammered.

"I offered him tea, but he didn't want any," Katy informed him.

"You are wanted at Morley House, sir. Immediately."

Philip frowned. "What does he want?"

The footman fidgeted, looked at the children, looked back at him again. "His Grace is dying, my lord."

Sitting in the velvet cushion of the carriage, it occurred to Philip that he could've just declined to come. His grandfather was nothing to him.

And yet.

Yet, he was his grandfather.

The carriage stopped in front of the ducal house. He

could get out and walk away. He stepped out of the carriage, and the door of the house opened. He climbed up the stairs.

He found himself in the vestibule. He took the stairs up.

Doors opened; people stepped away to let him through.

He was in the bedroom.

The four-poster bed was massive, swathed by heavy brocade curtains.

"My lord. We have to expect the worst," someone murmured, probably the doctor.

Philip looked at the figure in the gigantic bed. He felt his antagonism drain away. This was a lonely old man. Frail and shrunken. The white skin papery thin.

He opened his eyes with difficulty. His lips formed some words. There was no sound, but Philip understood.

"Grandfather," he said as he knelt next to his bed.

CHAPTER 31

"Oh, I wish that supper were already over." Lucy groaned. She was sitting on her desk scribbling the seating order. "Do I put Grandmamma next to Billingstone, or do you think they will kill each other?"

The Dowager Duchess Augusta loathed formal dinners and tended to verbally assassinate her table partners. Other than that, she got along surprisingly well with Lucy. At times, Arabella was somewhat jealous of their relationship.

"If I put her next to Conway, she will be bored out of her mind and refuse to attend any suppers the next few weeks. And I have to make an impression on that politician who is coming to speak specifically to Ash. Ugh, how I hate those political suppers. They bore me to tears."

"You can always bring in Bart to liven things up." Little Bartimaeus was their three-legged puppy who'd grown to a sleek, lively dog.

Lucy placed her elbow on the table and supported herself on it. "I still want to purchase a monkey from the travelling players. I feel terrible for them. The monkeys, not the players. They get mistreated. I was thinking I could save them if I buy them all. Henry won't mind, he doesn't know what to do with all his money anyway."

"Funny how all these animals take to Ash." A weak smile flitted over Arabella's face.

Lucy laughed. "He pretends he doesn't care for them, but he does. Deeply. He almost cried when Bart fell sick several months ago." Lucy smiled fondly. "He stayed next to her under his desk for hours and would've slept there, too, if Brown hadn't told him he'd take over the watch." Brown was Ashmore's secretary. "But back to a more imminent problem. This stupid table placement."

Lucy shook her head, shuffled the cards, froze. "Oh!" She picked up a card, her hand covering her mouth.

Arabella stared at the golden letters.

The Duke of Morley, it said in golden cursive.

Philip.

One morning, Lucy had wordlessly shown her an announcement that said that the old duke had passed away. Philip was now the new duke.

Arabella had been shaken.

"Henry mentioned he had something political to discuss with some people, but he might've mentioned that he'd invited him. He's declined, though. He's still in mourning. Have you heard from — him?"

"No." Arabella stared blindly at the card. She hadn't heard a single word. It was as though she'd never met Philip and his children. She'd been throwing herself into a wide range of activities, trying to forget.

Arabella shook away her thoughts and roused herself. "No. I haven't heard from them at all."

Lucy reached out for her hand. "I'm so sorry."

"It's no matter, Lucy. Really." Arabella's smile never reached her eyes.

Arabella tried to postpone the moment of going down to greet the guests. She'd even played with the thought of telling them she was indisposed. A headache, maybe. But then there'd be an unequal number of ladies to gentlemen, and that wouldn't reflect well on the hostess, Lucy.

Arabella sighed. Her abigail helped her put on her golden satin dress and fixed her hair. Then she went downstairs.

The guests were gathered in the blue drawing room. Arabella entered with a polite smile plastered on her face. She scanned the crowd. Everyone was gathered around one tall figure, clad in black.

Arabella froze.

Her heart started to thump slowly, then faster, until it filled her ears. She barely heard her brother say in that bored drawl of his, "Ah, Arabella. Look who is here."

She already knew. Her heart told her with every slow agonising beat.

"Lady Arabella." She had goosebumps at the sound of his voice.

She stood in front of him, staring at the white frills of his cravat. "Mr Merivale." Her voice shook.

"He is the Duke of Morley, now, Arabella. Remember?" Lucy said.

Only now she noticed the black band of mourning on his sleeve. "My condolences. You are a duke now."

He grimaced. "It seems it can't be helped."

The rusty voice of the Dowager Duchess Augusta spoke up. "Yes. Yes. These days dukes are raining from the sky. It is really quite incredible. Never has England been populated with so many dukes. One wonders where they all come from." She sniffed. Turning to Lucy she said, "Child. Are we to starve here or do you intend to feed us, eventually?"

"Supper's ready, Grandmamma. Shall we go in?"

The dowager's eyes roamed. "I shall sit next to that young

popinjay over there. He looks amusing." She pointed to a middle-aged man with a burgundy waistcoat, thereby completely oversetting Lucy's table placements.

Lucy threw up her hands. "As you wish." Then her eyes flitted from Arabella to Philip. "You'll take Arabella in to supper, of course," she told Philip. As the highest-ranking guest, he'd normally have to take in Lucy.

They ate the first two courses in awkward silence, listening to the main talk at the table, politics. Philip fumbled with the utensils, and once or twice, Arabella tapped inconspicuously at the right fork to guide him.

Arabella fiddled with her food and had no appetite whatsoever.

Neither did Philip. He fidgeted and used the napkin to wipe his forehead instead of his mouth.

"How are the children?" she murmured in–between two bites of venison.

"Fine." That came out as a croak. He cleared his throat. "They're fine."

Silence.

Table conversation had switched to the Peterloo affair. Arabella couldn't care less. She felt like she was having her own Peterloo disaster right here, right now.

"Your inventions?" Arabella asked. Never before had they conversed so stiffly.

He grimaced. "Declined."

Arabella's eyes flew to his face. "Oh. I'm so sorry."

He took a big gulp from his wine. "Don't be. It looks like I'm a tad too late with the patenting. Someone else was faster. It's called a *velocipede*. It's not a bad name, actually. Better than Two-Wheeler."

"Still, all the time and work you invested in it."

He smiled suddenly, and she caught her breath. "I got another patent. For the mechanical pencil. It is odd. I never intended to patent it, but it got through in record time. The interest is immense. Strange how things work sometimes."

"Yes, strange," Arabella echoed.

Their eyes met. She was drowning in a sea of green. Someone had removed her plate, and she hadn't even noticed that she was eating fish in aspic now.

"Morley?" Ashmore had to call him three times, before both snapped out of it.

Arabella said, "He means you."

"Dash it." Philip blinked as if aware of his surroundings only now. "I'll never get used to this."

"I was asking whether you agree that parliamentary representation needs to be reformed, Duke, but you seemed engaged." Ashmore lifted an eyebrow.

"Engaged." Philip sat up straight and gripped his fork. Then he blurted out: "Ashmore. I have the honour of asking for your sister's hand in marriage."

Dead silence fell over the table.

"Splendid. A marriage proposal in the middle of the third course. Haven't had one of those in a while." The Dowager Duchess Augusta looked from Philip to Arabella, clear enjoyment on her face.

Ashmore narrowed his eyes. "My dear fellow. This is neither the time nor place to talk about marriage to my sister."

"I disagree."

Ashmore was about to contradict when Lucy intervened. "But have you asked Arabella yet?"

"I am asking now." His eyes bored into hers.

"Really, Morley, this is unorthodox. I must insist you choose a more circumspect environment for your marriage proposals." Ashmore threw down his napkin.

"Is it plural, now?" The dowager cackled.

"I should very much like to marry you, Philip." Arabella

heard her own voice say quietly. She looked up with a bright red face from her wine glass, which she'd stared into the last few moments. Unbearable, this entire situation, unbearable. She heard her chair crash to the ground as she jumped up and fled. Up the stairs, to her room, and threw herself on to her bed. Where she cried.

Lucy joined her after a few minutes. She felt her hand on her hair, patting her gently. "You don't have to marry him, if you'd rather not."

Arabella looked up with a wet face, groping for a hand-kerchief. "Oh, but I do." She fell around Lucy's neck. "I really do. I am so happy, and I so very much want to marry him."

Ashmore and Philip had had their "talk" in the library, while the others had tea. It had been a short, blunt affair.

"I am not asking for your permission, Ashmore. I am placing you in front of an incontrovertible fact." Philip jutted out his chin. He'd been ready to fight. But Ashmore surprised him.

He'd steepled his fingers and given him one of his steel looks. "What makes you think that?"

"I love her." After a charged pause, he added. "I am certain she loves me, too."

He'd expected to be mocked. But he wasn't. Ashmore had nodded, which took the wind out of his sails. "I know." Then he'd gotten up and slapped him on the back. "You'd better make her happy."

And that had been that. They'd re-joined the company after five minutes, where everyone congratulated him.

Philip was in a daze.

Footmen were serving champagne now, to celebrate the occasion.

"I say, Ashmore, are your political suppers always this

entertaining?" asked the Viscount of Wilmore. He was the man with the burgundy waistcoat who was the Dowager Duchess' table partner.

"I try my best, Wilmore. Though I must say, this was one of my tamer affairs." He took the snuff that Wilmore offered him. "We once had a live squirrel entertain us."

"Egad. A squirrel!" Wilmore broke out laughing.

A smile crossed Ashmore's face and he met Lucy's eyes.

Philip decided that Ashmore was a man of unknown depths. Maybe they'd be able to get along, after all.

AFTER SHE'D WASHED HER FACE, DRIED IT, AND REARRANGED her curls, Arabella re-joined the company in the drawing room, where the guests had assembled. Strained conversation filled the room. Arabella's heart leapt when she saw Philip talk earnestly to her grandmamma. She went to him and stood next to him. Philip broke off and smiled.

"Let's take a walk," Arabella suggested.

They stepped out on the terrace. The cool night brushed her skin, but she didn't shiver.

"I should've asked you long before, of course. I was such an oaf." Philip turned to her. "Do you mind that I didn't propose the traditional way? Getting down on my knees. Rings and all that. You know I never do things the way one ought." He pulled his hand through his already mussed hair.

"I'd mangle it up hopelessly anyway."

Arabella laughed. "That is why I love you so."

He took both her hands. "You are my world. I must have fallen in love with you since I found you half-drowned under that tree."

Arabella chuckled and leaned her head against his shoulder. "I knew since that time at the lake. No. Probably before." She pointed up. "Oh! Look!"

The night sky exploded in fireworks.

"Blast." Philip tensed up immediately. She shook his arm gently and murmured soothing words.

He relaxed.

"Ash trying to celebrate the occasion, I suppose," Arabella said wryly.

"One day I will invent fireworks that don't boom," Philip vowed.

Arabella laughed. Then a thought occurred to her. "Do the children know? About us, I mean."

He nodded. "They badgered me to death. If I don't send them a positive message, they will come and storm the house."

"It would be lovely to have them here."

The fireworks tuned down, with a few remaining glimmers lightening up the night sky. It was magical.

Philip bent down, cupped her face in his hands. Arabella's entire body tingled.

His lips came coaxingly down on hers. She quivered at the sweet tenderness of the kiss. The entire world receded, and there was only him.

Afterwards, he held her in a tight embrace.

Arabella chuckled.

"What, my dear?" She felt his lips brush the fine hair on her temple.

"I just remembered something." She smiled. "That wishing well. Remember I told you about it? I wished that each of of us, myself and my friends, marries a duke. Now look at me. Marrying a duke."

"Was that what you wished for? Truly?"

She nodded. "Afterwards, I thought it was the greatest folly ever. Who would have known wishes come true after all?"

"I'd like to see that well one day," Philip remarked.

"You will. We shall have to send Katy to Miss Hilversham, Philip. She will love it there."

"Yes. And Joy, too. Eventually."

"After we're married, I will still continue my project regarding the reform of female education, you know. Now more than ever!"

"That is a splendid idea, my love. Can I come in and teach them the mathematical principles behind a steam-powered aircraft? I am convinced aeronautics is our future."

Arm in arm, they walked back into the drawing room.

EPILOGUE

"*A* letter for you, Your Grace." The footman held out a silver platter to Lucy.

The last few days had been strenuous, with an official engagement party and a ball, followed by invitations from all and sundry who were eager to congratulate the future Duchess of Morley. The children had joined them immediately and were now playing with Bartimaeus on the lawn.

The two dukes, Henry and Philip, had overcome their antagonism for each other. Philip gesticulated with both arms as he tried to convince Ashmore of installing a new pipe system in his house which would enable them standing baths and flushing toilets. It was revolutionary, he insisted. He'd be the first to be able to boast such an improvement in the house. Ashmore looked thoughtful and nodded occasionally. He was carrying baby Isolde, who was restless and teething.

Philip, at one point, had simply taken the baby from his arm and bumped her up and down on his own arm. He knew how to handle babies. After all, he'd raised three himself.

Isolde liked that and cooed. "I will invent a special teething toy for you," he promised her.

Arabella smiled as she saw the two men, with the baby, walk towards the rose garden. Lucy folded up a letter with a frown. "This is from Birdie."

"What does she write?" Arabella hadn't heard from Birdie in months.

Lucy frowned. "It sounds so odd." She flipped the paper over. "Not only is her normally impeccable handwriting almost illegible, but she also doesn't sound like herself." She handed Arabella the letter.

Arabella perused the letter.

"What do you think it means?"

"Dearest Lucy, when you receive this, know that I am fine and everything will be well. I just want you to know that. You, Arabella and Pen are my dearest friends, and I will never, ever *forget you. Yours, with great affection, Birdie."*

"How excessively odd!" Arabella took the letter from her and perused it. "It sounds like a goodbye letter."

"You are right. I am getting worried." Lucy's face was pale.

"What is even odder is that it was not delivered from Bath. Nor from her new position. Where is she teaching again?"

"Somewhere near Manchester, I thought."

"Look at this." Arabella pointed to the inked letters stamped on the back that clearly read "Inverness Penny Post."

"Inverness! Inverness is in —"

"Scotland!" Arabella jumped up. "What is she doing there?"

A slow smile spread over Lucy's face. "It looks like our sensible Birdie is finally getting herself into her very own adventure."

MEANWHILE, IN THE WISHING WELL AT 24 PARADISE ROW, TWO coins glittered mysteriously in the moonlight.

DON'T MISS BIRDIE'S AND GABRIEL'S STORY IN *BIRDIE AND THE Beastly Duke*!

NOTE BY THE AUTHOR

Because this is a work of fiction, I took some creative liberty regarding the actual dates of the inventions mentioned in this book. Philip, of course, was ahead of his time, as many engineering inventions did not take off until the Victorian Age.

His great invention that he failed to get patented was known as a "pedestrian curricle," or "Dandy horse," which was a forerunner of the bicycle, minus pedals and breaks. It was invented by Karl von Drais in 1817 Mannheim, Germany. By 1819, it was mass produced by Denis Johnson in London and grew rapidly in popularity.

The first mechanical pencil with a lead–propelling mechanism was patented by Sampson Mordan and John Isaac Hawkins in 1822.

Jean-Pierre Blanchard crossed the English Channel in 1785, from Dover to Calais. Ballooning was highly popular during the Victorian Era. I like to imagine that Robin would've taken an active part in it. Maybe he even had a hand in inventing the first aeronautical machine?

The American *SS Savannah* was indeed the first steamship

to cross the Atlantic, arriving in Liverpool in June 1819. It used steam for the first half of the trip and sails for the second.

Lastly, showers and flushing water closets were invented earlier than we think! By 1810, the first pump-based regency showers appeared, and Joseph Bramah patented flushing water closets already in 1780.

ALSO BY SOFI LAPORTE

The Wishing Well Series
Lucy and the Duke of Secrets
Arabella and the Reluctant Duke
Birdie and the Beastly Duke
Penelope and the Wicked Duke

Wishing Well Seminary Series
Miss Hilversham and the Pesky Duke

A Regency Christmas
A Mistletoe Promise

Merry Spinsters, Charming Rogues Series
Lady Ludmilla's Accidental Letter

ABOUT THE AUTHOR

Sofi was born in Vienna, grew up in Seoul, studied Comparative Literature in Maryland, U.S.A., and lived in Quito with her Ecuadorian husband. When not writing, she likes to scramble about the countryside exploring medieval castle ruins, which she blogs about here. She currently lives with her husband, 3 trilingual children, a sassy cat and a cheeky dog in Europe.

Get in touch and visit Sofi at her Website, on Facebook or Instagram!

a amazon.com/Sofi-Laporte/e/B07N1K8H6C
f facebook.com/sofilaporteauthor
twitter.com/Sofi_Laporte
instagram.com/sofilaporteauthor
BB bookbub.com/profile/sofi-laporte